On Trial For My Country

On Trial For My Country

John Thompson

STANLAKE SAMKANGE

HEINEMANN

Heinemann Educational Books Ltd
48 Charles Street, Mayfair, London W.1
PMB 5205, Ibadan; POB 25080, Nairobi

MELBOURNE   TORONTO   AUCKLAND
HONG KONG

PR
9390.9
S2
O5

Printed in Great Britain by
Western Printing Services Ltd, Bristol

Contents

Acknowledgments

Thanks are due to the British Museum for permission to reproduce the map which appears inside the front and back covers. The map first appeared in *The Financial News* of 18 October 1893, and was based on one issued by Rhodes' Chartered Company.

Thanks are also due to John R. Freeman and Co. (Photographers Ltd.) for the photograph of Lobengula which appears on the jacket; and to the Hulton Picture Library for that of Rhodes.

Chapter 9 closely follows Frank Johnson's own account of the Pioneer Corps in his book *Great Days*, to which the author is indebted.

Author's Preface

The Matebele are an offshoot of the Zulu people who, under Tshaka, occupied what is today Natal and Zululand in the Republic of South Africa. Mzilikazi, their first king, was one of Tshaka's most able and successful generals as well as chief of the Khumalo tribe. After accusing him of failing to surrender all the cattle he had taken in war, Tshaka personally led an *impi* against Mzilikazi who showed his mettle by standing up to the king until he was betrayed by one of his men and routed.

With the remnants of his army, Mzilikazi fled north and for a while settled in the Transvaal until a skirmish with the Boers compelled him to trek further north; conquering tribes along his way and incorporating their young into his regiments as soldiers and slaves—*Amahole*—until in 1840 he settled in what is today Matebeleland.

In this land Mzilikazi found that the Amakalanga (a tribe who, with numerous others, spread throughout what is today Mashonaland) had paid tribute to Rozwi rulers known as Mambo. Fortunately for Mzilikazi his kinsman Zwangendaba had preceded him and broken up the Rozvi power, defeating their king, Rupengo, at eNtaba ZikaMambo. Thus when Mzilikazi came on to the scene the various tribes which had formed the Rozwi Empire were leaderless and without a central authority. The Matebele entry into the country was therefore not only unchallenged but they were also able to extend their authority by conquering one tribe after another with ease.

Lobengula, second and last of the Matebele kings, claimed that his rule extended as far as his impis had marched. In fact, the Matebele proper were grouped in military kraals within a sixty-mile radius of their capital city—Bulawayo; it being considered unwise, from a military point of view, to have them scattered over a wider area. There were, nevertheless, tribes outside this area who recognized Matebele suzerainty and regularly paid tribute in grain, tobacco, etc., or were made custodians of the king's cattle. It is therefore impossible to draw a map with precise boundaries of the extent of the Matebele state; although such maps, drawn by concessionaires who had an interest in representing Lobengula as sovereign of a much larger area of Africa than that over which he ruled, exist. Perhaps it is more correct to speak in terms of a Matebele sphere of influence rather than in terms of boundaries.

Mzilikazi died in 1868 and Lobengula succeeded him as king in March 1870. Even before Mzilikazi's death European powers—Britain, Portugal, Germany—as well as the Transvaal Republic were casting envious eyes on Mzilikazi's lands which they believed were rich in gold. How and why Cecil J. Rhodes, representing British interests, succeeded not only in preventing his European rivals from entering the country but also in taking the country from the Matebele king in 1893, is the burden of this story.

I am indebted to my wife for compiling the glossary, and to my sons, Stanlake and Harry, in spite of whose efforts this book was completed.

Bloomington, Indiana, U.S.A.　　　　　　　　S. J. T. SAMKANGE
January 1966

CHAPTER ONE

Prelude

Whenever I am in Bulawayo, I always make it a point to attend the three o'clock service at the Methodist Church in the Old Location. There are several reasons for this. My father was thrice a minister of that church, first from 1928 to 1930, then from 1934 to 1936, and it was while he was serving his third term that he died suddenly of a heart attack on 27 August 1956. Perhaps because of this, there is a special significance in the welcome which particularly the older members of this church extend to me when I go there. 'Come and meet your father's class-meeting,' one of them will say, after the service, and what these old people say to me on these occasions never fails to penetrate to my heart.

I was only six years old when my family first occupied the Methodist Manse at the Old Location and yet, even now, I still remember clearly the day we arrived. There are many things I also remember. I remember my playmates—Samson Gwala, Amon Dhliwayo, David (Puffy) Nkipa and many others. I remember my teacher, Mr George Kaluwa, the charts we used to read or, to be more exact, recite; the games we played at school; our dramatization of stories from the Bible, and when I played the part of David in the story of

1

David and Goliath; the concerts we had; the red and yellow uniforms we wore at these concerts; the singing at our school and when our school won and brought to our home the first inter-school singing trophy ever presented in the Location. I remember the singing in the church on Sundays, the old man uMzizi and one before him, who kept the congregation's singing from 'dragging' by beating, with the palm of the hand, on one part of the pulpit until it became smooth and its paint wore off. I remember the chanting of the Responses for they never appeared ever to be coming to an end. I remember the singing of the old man uMdhlongo for he bellowed like a bull and made it quite impossible for anyone else to be heard. I remember the comfortable red cushions that were spread on the steps to the pulpit because on them I usually stretched myself and was often sound asleep until the sermon was over. I remember those large beautiful red letters which were written high upon the wall across the pulpit—UTIXO ULUTANDO. These letters can no longer be seen today because some poor devil took it into his head to erase them when he was told to whitewash the walls. I confess that many a time I have gone into this church, and instead of listening to the preacher's exhortations, I have tried still to see these letters beneath the several layers of whitewash over them. Once or twice, I think I succeeded in seeing them.

Thus it was that on this Sunday afternoon, the service over, I as usual renewed acquaintances and exchanged pleasantries with quite a number of people, many of whom I had not seen for some time. I then got into my car to go to Luveve when an idea suddenly seized me, that I should, instead, drive thirty miles to Mzingwane School near Essexvale and call on my friends there. Without giving the matter further thought, I yielded to the impulse and drove out of that Mission gate as I must have done hundreds of times before, drove straight on for a few hundred yards, then turned left before I got to the clinic, went past the Salvation Army building, past the 'Matumbu Butchery' across the old football ground to the macadamized road near the Stanley Hall. I crossed over to Sixth Avenue Extension, turned left towards Lobengula Street and downtown. At Fort Street I turned right and then turned left again into Selbourne Avenue which leads one out to Essexvale and on to Johannesburg.

I must have thought about half a dozen different things as I drove out. I remember distinctly, however, that I mused over the fact that the car I was driving then, an almost new Ford Galaxie, was, to put it mildly, a lot better than the little old and ramshackle Ford Prefect 'chova mubayiwa' I ran when I worked at Mzingwane. Then, a trip to or from town, during which there was no puncture, or brakes failing, or the petrol line closing or the starter being jammed, or the lights failing, or the points misfiring, or the carburettor and plugs having to be cleaned on the way or the car just refusing to budge, was so rare that when it happened, I would for days exultingly tell my friends, 'I came back from town and didn't have any trouble with the car!'

I was thinking about all this when I realized that I had been driving for over thirty minutes and should have been near e Danger now. I stopped, examined the countryside carefully and came to the conclusion that I was not on the road to Essexvale but on some strange road with which I was not familiar. I decided to turn back. In reversing the car, however, it slipped into a ditch, which I had not seen, by the side of the road. I spent the next thirty minutes or so trying to get the car out of the ditch without success.

The sun was descending the sky and I knew that soon it was going to be dark. I did not wish to be alone, in the dark, on a strange road. I tried once more to start the engine and to get the car out of the ditch but this time the starter would not even work. I pulled the lights' switch—there were no lights. I checked on the battery terminals and found them intact, but the starter would not turn, neither would the lights switch on. 'Only oxen can pull this car out of this ditch and I'll need another battery to drive it to town,' I told myself. So I looked around for a village where I could get help.

Some distance away, among the trees, I saw what appeared to be a number of huts and beyond were clearly the Matopo Hills; for the first time I realized where I was—nearing the Matopos. I walked towards the huts. I walked for about an hour but did not appear to get anywhere nearer those huts. They seemed to recede as I advanced towards them. I walked on and on, wondering how I could ever have missed the road to Essexvale—a road on which I had driven hundreds of times before and can tell blindfolded. I wondered how I had let the car slip into that ditch and why I had not noticed it. I wondered how a good battery could have gone flat so quickly so much so that it had no power left to turn the starter or lights on.

I found myself among the hills and was about to decide to return to the car since it was beginning to get dark, when suddenly I saw a fire burning only a few yards away. I stopped. My heart beat faster, my hair stood stiff, there was sweat on my neck and my knees shook in my trousers. I was petrified with fear.

I saw a man, an old man, sitting by the fire at the mouth of a cave. His eyes were fixed on the burning logs but somehow I felt that he had long been watching me. I wanted to run away but I did not have the strength to run. I found myself walking towards him as if I were not afraid. When I was about fifteen yards away, I stopped and shouted, 'May I enter, my father?' in accordance with the custom of the

4

Amandebele which requires one to announce oneself before one enters a village. Without even lifting his eyes to me, the man replied, 'Yes, Ngwenya, enter son of Mfundisi, enter son of Samkange.'

My fear melted into wonder and amazement. How did this man know me or my name? I had never seen him before. His reply, nevertheless, made me feel somewhat easy and encouraged me to approach him without being paralysed by fear.

I came nearer and then sat down, for it is considered bad manners to greet people, particularly people older than oneself, while one is standing.

'I greet you, my father!' I said.

'I greet you, Ngwenya,' he replied, for the first time lifting his eyes to me.

'How are you, my father?' I said.

'I am well, Ngwenya, as well as I can be, for my days have passed and they are arriving who come to take me.'

'How do we know each other, my father? Have we met before, since my father appears to know me and the one who bore me?'

'Yes, I knew your father. I saw him often when I lived in town many years ago. We like him well.'

'I see, my father has a keen eye for resemblances. I did not know that anyone could tell I was Samkange's son simply by looking at me.'

'Oh, you look very much like your father. Even your voice is like his. Anyway, that is not the way I recognized you, because I brought you here.'

'You brought me here? I do not understand, my father.'

'There are many things you do not understand, Ngwenya. Is it not true that you left town intending to go to Mzingwane School?'

'It is true, my father.'

5

'Is it not true that you have had trouble with your car and need help?'

'That is also true, my father.'

'How is it, then, that you are on this road, for this road is far from the road to Essexvale?'

'I do not know, my father. I believed I was on the road to Essexvale until I thought I should have, by then, been at e Danger. That is when I realized I was lost.'

'Yes, you do not know. I called you and led you here. You would never have found this place on your own. I have lived here for some time now, and yet you are the first person to come here. I have called you here because I have words I want you to know. Words that many other people should know.'

'I thank my father for trusting me with a message but may I ask what made him choose me?'

'I chose you because I wanted somebody who will tell this "matter" to many people and I know you can do this well, son of Samkange.'

'I hear you, my father, although my father has not told me his name.'

'Yes, my name is Gobinsimbi, the son of Dabulamanzi, of the house of Khumalo, but men call me Mafavuke now. I was not born in this part of the country. I was born far away among the Mopane forests near the banks of the Shangani River. I came to the city as a boy and have never returned to my home. I worked in the city for many years and when I grew too old to work I came and lived among the people here and then died.'

'Did my father say, died?'

'Yes, I said, died. I died.

'Although none of these people here are related to me, I had lived well among them for a number of years so they sincerely mourned my death and prepared to give me a de-

6

cent funeral. They had already washed me and put me in the coffin and were about to take me to the grave when I returned from the dead. Many of them were terrified and almost died of fear, others ran away from the village and have not, to this day, returned. I decided that it was better for me to leave the village and live alone here where I would frighten no one. But my time is approaching again. I must return to join my ancestors once more.'

'Does my father tell me that he actually died, and is alive again?'

'You appear to be surprised by what I say Ngwenya. Do you mean to say that this is the first time you have heard that a person in this country died and rose up again?'

I thought for a while and then replied, 'Now that my father has asked me, I find, I must say, that it is common, in this country, to hear people talk of someone who died and rose from the dead.

'I remember a man, of the Nenguo people, whose name was Bangamuseve. Men said that it was after he rose from the dead that he became a great Evangelist converting many people to the Christian faith. I also remember a man who was called Dividzwa, at Chikaka in the Zwimba tribal area. People said this man died and they prepared to bury him. In accordance with their custom they broke his legs, before wrapping him in a skin. Then this man returned from the dead. I knew him. I saw his broken legs. After that, he was named Lazarus. Then there is the case, more recently, of Mai Chaza who has thousands upon thousands of followers in the country today. I heard her declare that she had died and returned from the dead to do more work for God. No, now that I have thought about it, my father, it is not strange that you say you died and returned from the dead.'

'Indeed, it is not strange, Ngwenya. Yes, I was dead for several days. I saw that which I saw and heard that which I heard and returned to tell my tale. That is why I called you here—to tell you what I saw and heard so that you can tell it to those who have ears to hear.'

'I hear you my father, Khumalo.'

Thus it was that the old man told me his tale which I will repeat as simply as he told it to me. I speak only the words he spoke. The voice that you hear is mine but the words that come out of my mouth are his.

Listen then, ye that have ears, to the true tale and words of Gobinsimbi, the son of Dabulamanzi of the house of Khumalo, whom men now call uMafavuke, as I heard them by a fire, at the mouth of a cave, somewhere on the Matopo Hills.

CHAPTER TWO

The Great Indaba

When I sank and passed away from life on this earth, I had no sooner joined the spirits of my forefathers in the life of the hereafter than I immediately realized that something unusual and important was about to take place, for assembled in Council, right in front of my eyes, were all the great of the Amandebele nation. It was a most magnificent sight to behold, a sight whose splendour, solemnity and dignity blended to swell my breast with pride as I saw all the greatest heroes of our nation still wearing the elegant plumes, head rings and kilts which, as mortal men, marked their rank and station in the land. Once more the Amandebele kings and indunas were holding a national indaba, beneath the immortal indaba tree, as in the past! Noiselessly and without attracting the attention of anyone, I joined them.

Then uMncumbata, the lifelong friend and spokesman for the Elephant uMzilikazi, the trusted induna who had acted as regent during the Elephant's last days on earth and later nominated the Lion uLobengula, king, addressed the gathering saying:

'Bayete! My Lord the Bull Elephant and Eater of Men; the Noble Lion uLobengula and my fathers. It is our custom, when we hear great cases concerning the welfare of the nation, for the king to be present in person. It is not our custom, however, that the king himself should conduct the proceedings. That is my humble duty as the king's mouth, eyes, and ears. Today, it will be necessary for us to depart from this custom because the one who is sitting here before us—and who will answer all our questions is not only a son of our royal father the Elephant uMzilikazi—son of Matshobana, Matshobana of Mangete, Mangete of Langa; but is himself a king—the Lion, uLobengula last King of the Amandebele—the Great Lion whose knees are still red; red, because of kneeling on the blood of men. It is he who will answer and throw light on the plight of our people—the Amandebele of Mzilikazi, Mzilikazi the Great Elephant of Matshobana.

'It is not, therefore, proper for me, a mere mouth, though spokesman of the Great and Noble Elephant, to direct questions to the king. I must leave it to the Elephant, his father, to ask the questions and conduct the hearing.

'The Noble Elephant wishes his son, the Lion uLobengula, to say, before you all, how he looked after the inheritance left him by his father—the people, the cattle and the land for which many of us here fought, bled and died. Where are the Amandebele today? Where are their slaves—the Amahole? Who owns their land? Whose cattle graze and grow fat in the valleys of the land? Who rules the land? And why? These, my fathers, are some of the questions the Elephant will ask of the Lion: questions which, no doubt, you have all been asking in your hearts but could find no adequate answers, for what answers you could find were as distasteful as they were incredible. The Great Elephant will now trumpet and the Noble Lion roar.'

There were murmurs of approval, nodding of heads and mutterings of 'we hear you Mncumbata', as the 'mouth' of the Elephant, uMzilikazi spoke and when he finished all clapped their hands in applause, many with tears running down their cheeks.

Then slowly sitting up, so that his bare buttocks came closest to the stretching root of the indaba tree allowing his upturned hind 'bechu' to protect his wrinkled loose skin as his back rested perpendicularly, as far as the shoulders, against the erect trunk of the tree; his front 'bechu' neatly falling between his long black thighs resting on his earthen stool; his feet, in cow-hide sandles, firmly planted on the ground; his right hand tightly grasping an erect spear; his sharp piercing eyes, staring at his son in sorrow, pity and love not unmixed with anger, disdain, and disappointment; Mzilikazi, looking in every way a king, opened his mouth and in a clear firm voice said, 'My son, my heart sinks with sorrow and pain to see what my people are today. No more does the sun rise on the glittering glory of the sharp spears of the Amandebele marching to do battle in yonder mountains. No more does fear of the Amandebele impis make the Amahole sleep like squirrels, huddled up in caves with their cattle and goats. The valleys of the mountains echo the thudding hoofs of a thousand, thousand Amahole cattle on their way to Amandebele kraals no more; Amahole women and children are no more our slaves.

'Instead, the Amandebele have become the Amahole—the slaves of the whiteman. They are now scattered all over the land like the dry leaves of a tree in autumn and like the leaves of a tree they only live to fall down, die and be buried.

'Did we flee along a trail of blood from Tshaka's wrath, across swollen rivers and thick forests, fighting and conquering man, Boer and beast to come here and be slaves of the whiteman?

'Now speak, Lobengula, and say what happened. When I joined the spirits of our fathers our kraals were full of cattle and our granaries stacked with corn. Our wives grew fat with feasting and our children strong with playing. Our majaha only fought and danced. Both the Abelungu and the

11

Amahole feared the spear of the Amandebele but today the Abelungu and the Amahole treat the Amandebele like a lion that has no teeth.

'Some say that you sold the country for a few pieces of gold, useless guns and for an even more worthless gunboat on the Zambezi. Is this true?

'You were present at emHlahlandlela when a delegation of Boers led by uJani Viljoen, an elephant hunter, begged me to sell my land at Tati to their king uKruger. They told me that many whitemen would soon rush to that area to look for gold but if I sold the land to them they would prevent these whitemen from entering my country. Do you remember what I told them? I told them that I would not sell any part of my country or allow any other nation to settle within my borders. I told them that just as no two bulls can live in one kraal no two kings can rule in one country; and there would be no peace if whitemen were brought to live in the same country with blackmen. I told them to return whence they came. They did. No whiteman ever dug gold in my country as long as I lived. I never saw the great rush of whitemen to dig gold in my country that I had been told about.

'What witch, what wizard and what medicines then, could have made you sell my people, my cattle, and my land to these whitemen? No one knew the ways of witches and wizards better than you who ate and slept with them for many moons in the Matopo Hills. How, then, could anyone bewitch you to sell your birthright and lose your manhood? Speak, Lobengula.'

The old king closed his eyes and gripped his spear tighter. Small beads of perspiration ran down his forehead. With his left hand he wiped them off slowly and gently. For a moment he appeared to be lost in thought and oblivious of the presence of his companions. Was the effort of articulation too exhausting for him? Or, had the conflicting emotions he had betrayed momentarily burnt him up?

Perhaps sensing this his audience did not respond. There was no applause or grunts of approval. No nodding of the heads or clapping of hands. Only the silence—the deep silence of the grave. All eyes were fixed to the ground.

Then the old king opened his eyes. Lobengula raised his head. They looked each other straight into the eyes. It was clear from the expression on his face that Lobengula appreciated the gravity and magnitude of the charges levelled against him, and that in a very real sense, he was about to begin a battle in which he would have to fight harder than he had ever done against any mortal foe. For just as in the past he had engaged in battle and preserved himself—his body, from being killed, he was now going to engage in a verbal battle to clear his name and preserve his honour from being for ever besmirched and himself from being eternally condemned as one who sold to the whitemen for posterity a people, a country and a heritage left under his trusteeship.

Slowly he reached for his long staff that lay by his side, for although all the other men present had left their weapons outside in accordance with Matebele law which forbade them to carry arms in the presence of the king, Mzilikazi and Lobengula, because they were kings, had appeared, one with a spear and the other with a staff. With the help of his staff Lobengula stood up apologizing as he did so to his royal father, for standing up in his presence. Again, because Lobengula was a king, breach of the custom which required all men, unless otherwise directed, to remain seated or prostrate in the presence of the king, was overlooked.

All eyes were turned on Lobengula as he stood there holding his staff, a picturesque figure, tall, well built, and standing over six feet from the ground. A very stout man weighing over 280 pounds and yet, not unwieldy in his stoutness and in fact appearing smaller than he really was, because of his height. His body was a fine coppery-bronze in colour and scrupulously clean. His face was pleasant and good-tempered but also showed resoluteness and determination. He stood there, his head slightly thrown back and his broad chest expanded, proud, dignified and stately, every inch a king. He stood there naked, except for a thin roll of blue cloth round his waist and a sporran of monkey skins. A truly majestic figure, an imposing monarch and a man among men. He addressed the great indaba, saying:

'My noble father, the Bull Elephant, Eater of Men and gallant indunas of the Amandebele nation. When the Great Mountain, the loftiest in the land, fell and we laid him to eternal rest in a regal granite-walled cave in the Matopos, I, as an offspring of his noble loins did not wish, without him, to breathe the air he had breathed; to see the trees he had seen; the mountains he had scaled and the rivers he had crossed. All I prayed for was that since the spirits of our ancestors had neither accepted our sacrifices nor assisted the royal medicine men to rejuvenate the king, they should now let the sky fall upon the earth so that all things on earth may perish with the king.'

Murmurs of approval were heard from the audience as Lobengula continued.

'My prayers, like those of our priests, were ignored. The sky did not fall on the earth and the sun continued each day to rise in the east and set in the west. The gallant uMncumbata there invited me to take over the leadership of the nation as king, but I refused. I refused because, as I have said, I wished everything on earth to perish with the king, and also because I did not wish to involve the nation in a civil war with those who might have had a better claim to my father's stool than I.

14

'Indunas, Lotshe, Magaba, Mtanyelo, and Mhlaba went to Zululand and Natal to search for my brother Nkulumane, the heir apparent, and also to ask the governor there to send me a doctor and sea water. They could not find Nkulumane. I was again asked to become king and this time I agreed. I agreed because I saw that, in the absence of Nkulumane, there was no one with a better claim than mine, and furthermore, I had the support of all the leading indunas with the exception of Mbiko.

'Eighteen months after the falling of the mountain, I was installed king at emHlahlandlela. In accordance with our custom, I set about building a new capital at Bulawayo and uniting the people. Only Mbiko one of the bravest and ablest of my father's generals was uncooperative and defiant of my authority. For this, the indunas of the royal council sentenced him to death, but remembering the great battles he had fought and won as commander of the renowned and invincible Zwangendaba regiment and the outstanding contribution he had made in the conquest of our territories between the twin rivers of the Limpopo and the Zambezi, I refused to have him executed. Instead, I sent indunas to point out to him that we could never be a strong and fearful people as long as he remained defiant of my authority as king. Mbiko replied by thrashing my messengers and telling them to inform me that henceforth he would talk with spears alone.

'Most reluctantly I was forced to fight Mbiko and the Zwangendaba regiment and although they repulsed us twice we eventually defeated them and put Mbiko to death.

'Some time after this incident I received a messenger from the Governor of Natal who spoke these words:

The Governor of Natal thanks Lobengula the son of Mzilikazi for his friendly message; he receives it as the sentiments of the Matebele people; he also accepts the tusk of ivory Lobengula has sent as the proof of the sincerity of his words.

The Government of Natal is the largest native power in South Eastern Africa and its territory is the resort of refugees of all ranks from surrounding tribes. The Governor of Natal is looked upon as the father of all and hears what all have to say—he therefore is intimately acquainted with the domestic circumstances of surrounding populations—he does not seek for this information, it comes to him.

Among these refugees is a son of Mzilikazi. He has been recognized by a deputation of his own people to be their heir to the Matebele chieftainship for whom a fruitless search has been made ever since Mzilikazi's death. The Governor knows this from the position he holds. Acting therefore as becomes this position he has desired Lobengula's ambassador to see this son of their deceased Chief and to satisfy themselves of the truth or otherwise of his person—they can then take back with them a reliable report to Lobengula and the Matebele people on the subject.

The Governor does not wish to interfere with or influence any nation in the selection or appointment it may think proper to make of its future King, but he knows that it will be better hereafter for all parties concerned that such appointment should be decided upon after having acquired a full knowledge of all the circumstances.

Lobengula will therefore perceive that to send him a doctor such as his father had and the water from the great sea would, under the present state of things, mislead the Matebele people, so that they will be apt to believe that the Government of Natal has decided against one brother and is in favour of another and that such decision has been arrived at with a knowledge of the position and claims of both.

The Governor of Natal cannot accept such a position. He would be discharging but indifferently the duties devolving upon him as the head of many people if by concealment he should sow discord. For the Matebele to reap bloodshed and such would be the certain result, if after so grave an act as the permanent appointment by a nation of its King it became known to the people, as it must sooner or later, that such an act had been recommended, the representation that no trace of the true heir had been found when in fact the knowledge that a person existed who called himself the heir and who had been recognized as such by his eldest brother uMangwana and others of his people had been kept concealed from them. Let the ruling men of the land know all the truth and decide as they please with the full knowledge of the facts before them.

In giving this advice the Governor speaks as one willing to listen to all representations made to him and who is anxious to preserve peace and good feeling among all people.

The Governor of Natal will always be glad to hear of the happiness and prosperity of the Matebele, he acknowledges the hospitality and kindness with which they have always treated Englishmen and he trusts that the sentiment of respect which has prompted this treatment will never be wrecked or destroyed.

The Governor sends a few articles which he hopes may prove useful to Lobengula.

'To this message I replied as follows:

I, Lobengula, chief of the Amandebele Nation have to acknowledge the kind and friendly message brought to me by Mr Baines and I return you my best and most sincere thanks for the friendship and service you have rendered me, and hope that your Excellency will continue to favour me in the same manner when occasion may require.

With regard to the message your Excellency has sent me respecting a person said to be Nkulumane—I cannot now listen to it as I have reliable information from my own people that the true Nkulumane was not sent out in the usual manner but was killed in this country by order of Mzilikazi.

After the death of Mzilikazi there were two opinions in the country: the first that search should be made for Nkulumane, the other that he was dead. Search was accordingly made in every direction for Nkulumane and to such an extent that messengers from the Amandebele Nation reached Natal and saw the person to whom your Excellency refers and they declare that he was not the real man.

The Matebele then came to me and said, "You are, according to your birth, the next heir of your father uMzilikazi and we require you to take upon yourself the Chieftainship of our Nation." This request was made to me in the winter of 1869, about the month of July, and I declined to comply with it so long as there was a hope of Nkulumane being found.

I attempted to go out myself to search for my brother and I applied to Mr Jewell at Kumalo to give me guides and assistance to reach Natal but he did not feel himself at liberty to supply these in the absence of Mr Baines. All the white men know that I made every endeavour to find my brother and I refused the chieftainship until my people threatened that they would break up as a nation and disperse themselves amongst other tribes.

My father, uMzilikazi gave orders for the destruction of the kraal at Intab' ezindunda to which Nkulumane's mother belonged. I myself, being then a child, was in the village but was saved by Gwabalanda, induna of Mhlahlandhlela who hid me from the massacre.

It was however found that Nkulumane was not there but at the kraal of Zwangendaba and my father sent a Basutu named Gwabaiiyo to call him. He came with his servant Gwalema, who was not suspecting danger and uMzilikazi ordered the Basutu to take Nkulumane out and kill him. This Basutu is still living in this country. After this Gwabalanda had a very serious argument with Mncumbata asking him why he had advised or allowed uMzilikazi to kill Nkulumane and destroy his heir and hope of the Amandebele Nation.

After the death of Nkulumane Gwalema ran to Zwangendaba and reported the fact—then uMzilikazi sent for Moonto his son, and Mhlaba, Mncumbata's son, and had medicine given the maccording to Amandebele custom because their companion was killed.

Now when these witnesses Gwabaiiyo and Gwalema were called before the Council of the Nation in August 1869, Gwabaiiyo said the king's orders to him were "You must not stab him with an assegai, you must not bruise him with a kerrie, but you must take his head in your own hands and kill him by twisting his neck so as to dislocate it," and he said he killed him according to these orders.

Gwalema at the same time disputed the manner of Nkulumane's death and said Gwabaiiyo did not adhere to the orders of Mzilikazi but took bark off a tree, twisted it into rope and strangled him by twisting this about his neck and he also broke his kerrie in striking Nkulumane, but both agreed that he was put to death.

19

It was the younger people who thought that a search should be made but the older ones who knew the facts said, "How can one rise from the dead and be sent out of the country? With whom was he sent or could a child go so far, or pass through so many enemies as the late king must have made in his progress from eZansi?"

Mncumbata knew also from the first that Nkulumane was dead but nevertheless for the satisfaction of the nation he consented to the search; and now a letter was received that the person living there denied that he was Nkulumane but said that he had known him during his childhood.

When Elijah and Mr Levert came up they said they had seen him and questioned him about uButhuli a brother of Nkulumane who was killed at the kraal of Intab' ezindunda; he seemed to be perfectly ignorant of this and many other circumstances which the real Nkulumane must have known.

Up to the time when the testimony I have mentioned was brought before the Council of the Nation, I was myself one of those who doubted whether Nkulumane was not alive and I exerted myself to search for him. Before I applied to Mr Jewell I had already taken six attendants of whom uMlomenqaba, the induna of the Hlalini section of the Nqameni regiment, was one, and attempted to go out by way of Zoutpansberg. However I was taken ill on the road and was obliged to turn back, but I gave my party a black ox for provision on their way. They proceeded as far as the place of the Signor Abansini, a Portuguese who lived in the Spelonken area of the Northern Transvaal and there they were told it was unsafe for them to go farther as the tribes in advance were the enemies of the Amandebele.

When Mr Levert went down to Natal for the first time I also gave him a large ox in token of friendship and requested him to seek for Nkulumane because it was my brother and blood relationship that I wished to find. In the face of the testimony both from natives and whitemen of whom enquiries had been made, I could no longer refuse to comply with the request repeatedly made by my people and I consented to accept that dignity which after Nkulumane's death was mine by birthright.

In February of 1860, I was duly installed in the place of my father as Chief and King of the Amandebele Nation; 10,000 warriors were present at the ceremony and many more had paid homage and departed. A few remained disaffected but I was patient and said why should I kill my own people.

Although the Zwangendaba, the chief of the disaffected tribes had frequently made prisoners of men who were loyal to me and had actually killed two of them, I avoided all cause of quarrel as long as possible, but at length I was accused of having taken cattle belonging to Zwangendaba. I went to their village in person to deny the charge. I did not call up a regular army, but my people gathered and followed me of their own accord. As soon as the Zwangendaba saw me coming they armed themselves and prepared for war. I sent a messenger named Mhlatuzana, a petty chief, to say that I wished to speak to uMbiko the chief of the tribe, but uMbiko at once declared war and sent him back. I then went to speak in person, and as I came within range they fired on me from the village—the people who were with me had not even their war shields or dresses, but as soon as they saw me in danger they charged with the weapons they had to defend me.

After some partial repulses my people forced an entrance and defeated the rebels and as soon as victory was gained I gave orders that slaughter should cease and that no one should be killed after the battle was over, because my heart was not for blood. I did not want to shed more than I was compelled although the war had been forced upon me and I was obliged to fight to defend myself. The survivors I forgave freely and sent them into other regiments. I have now also subdued all other disaffected persons in my country and my nation is now at peace.

Your Excellency will see from what I have said how loath I was to accept the dignity of sovereign of my nation, but having once consented to do so, I must to the best of my power show myself worthy of the trust reposed in me and not lightly resign my high office.

I beg to assure your Excellency that I fully appreciate the just and proper course you have pursued in not taking part in the dispute which properly concerns the Matebele themselves, and in desiring the subjects of your great Queen to remain neutral; and I further beg of you not to give encouragement to the person calling himself Nkulumane to disturb the peace which now exists in my country by raising war and bloodshed in it.

I shall not begin war. I wish to remain at peace, but if I am attacked I shall defend myself as becomes the king of a nation of warriors like the Matebele.

I am a friend of whitemen. I am opening my country to them and I hope in years to come that lasting friendship and advantageous intercourse will be established between us.

I have again to thank your Excellency very much for the friendship you have shown to me and to the Amandebele nation in forwarding information and advice of so great importance to me and to them, and hoping that the friendship between the Amandebele and the British people will never be interrupted but increase as our intercourse becomes more general and frequent.

'After I had sent these words to the Governor of Natal, I never heard again of the person who called himself Nkulu-mane.

'The nation then settled down, united and strong. We lived very much as we had done during the reign of my father. We feasted, danced, and sent impis to conquer new tribes and to bring slaves, cattle and food. But one thing began to trouble us—whitemen. Whitemen started becoming regular visitors to the royal kraal asking for permission to hunt in the country and sometimes just to hang around. As in the days of my father, we kept an eye on them.

'One day, however, a Boer named Piet Grobler and his brother Frederick came to the royal kraal at Emganweni. They told me that they carried the greetings of their king uKruger who then ruled in the place of Potgieter with whom my father had signed a treaty of general friendship many years before. I remembered this treaty well. They then told me that the copy of the treaty my father had signed with Potgieter had been lost and now they wished me to sign one exactly like the one my father had signed. They gave me a paper and I signed it. One of them then asked me for an impi to fight Khama the King of the Bamangwato, and the other asked to be allowed to live in the country. I refused both requests.'

'Just pause for a moment, I wish to put some questions to you,' said the Elephant uMzilikazi.

'As my father pleases.'

'Had you not been advised that in your dealings with the whiteman, you must never sign anything because since you could not read what they wrote on their paper, you would not know what you were, in fact, signing?'

'I had been so advised, my father, and, as a matter of fact, until this occasion I had never agreed to sign anything.'

'Why then did you sign?'

'I signed because I thought I was merely doing what my father before me had done—merely renewing a treaty, signed by my father which had been lost.'

'You have answered well. Now, tell me, is it not true that this treaty you signed with Grobler went much further than my agreement with Potgieter and not only called for perpetual peace between the Amandebele and the Boers but also acknowledged you as an independent ally and bound you to help the Boers with troops when asked; to extradite offenders; to accept a resident consul and most important of all, to allow anyone with a pass from the King of the Boers to hunt or trade in your country?'

'If the treaty I signed contained all these things my father has said, then all I can say is that I never understood it to contain them. How could I have agreed to give away my country like that? Had I not refused one of the brothers an impi to fight Khama? How could I have agreed to help the Boers with troops and then immediately refuse to honour my word when asked for troops to fight Khama? Had I not refused to allow the other brother to reside in my country? How could I have agreed to accept a resident consul and then refuse permission the envoy of the person whose consul I had agreed to accept?'

'Well spoken. There is truth in your eyes.'

And with murmurs of 'Well spoken', 'He speaks true', and 'Never trust a whiteman!' from the audience, the royal council adjourned.

CHAPTER THREE

Rhodes' Creed

When the great royal indaba of the Amandebele adjourned, I looked across the seas and saw, in far-off England, at a place called Bishop's Stortford, a church. In the church, standing before the congregation was a person I recognized as Cecil John Rhodes—the man who, for a prize, a gigantic prize, had pitted his wit, wile and wealth against Lobengula. And the prize was my country. I decided to go there since, in the Hereafter, time, space and language barriers exist no more. There indeed was Cecil John Rhodes, standing before the congregation and facing his father who was in the pulpit. For this was his father's church—the place in and around which Rhodes had, as a boy, learnt the code of ethics he was enjoined to observe throughout his life on earth and by which he was, in the end, to be judged. The congregation was his father's spiritual flock, to whom the Rev. Francis William Rhodes was obliged to show, not only that he practised what he preached when he taught them to raise their children to fear the Lord and walk in His path but also that he had been more successful than they, in leading his own children along the paths of righteousness.

Thus, it was a somewhat worried Vicar of Bishop's Stortford who stood in his pulpit that day, ready, not to deliver his customary pungent ten-minute sermon but to ask his son Cecil to account for some of his actions in life and answer certain serious allegations that had been levelled against him.

'My son,' the tall, thin and scholarly-looking Vicar began, 'if fame and wealth were the sole criteria by which success in life was measured, you would stand here as the most successful boy from this parish and indeed, as one of the most successful sons of England. Few men in this world have enjoyed the honour and blessings which the Lord has allowed to be bestowed upon you. Two countries north and south of one of Africa's most majestic rivers—the Zambezi River, along which lies God's most beautiful and picturesque poem in water—the Victoria Falls or as the people of the land call it "Masi-wa-tunya—the smoke that thunders"—have been named after you. The dark, unfathomed caves of Africa have yielded to you their gems of purest ray serene in diamonds and gold and made you one of the wealthiest men on God's earth. And, as if this were not enough, you have been immortalized in the works of some of our most inspired men of letters.

'What have you done to thank the Lord for all these blessings? Some say you have, instead, unscrupulously dealt with other men and cheated them out of their money and land. Indeed, others say, as in the case of a Boer named Grobler, you planned the death of many and through your recklessness and greed for fame and fortune, caused even many more to die in unnecessary adventures, raids and wars.

'And more specifically, it is charged that by wile, guile, and other dishonourable methods such as corrupting a minister of the Gospel you drove an African monarch named Lobengula out of his country, usurped his land, burnt his kraals, massacred his people, took their cattle, and enslaved those of his subjects who survived.

'These are grievous allegations which, if true, would

26

remove from your life the honour and glory of success for which men admire and praise you. In your youth you were taught to live according to the law of Christ, the law of love, purity, honesty and unselfishness. As a Christian, by this law you will be judged. Can you say that in your dealings with other men, particularly the Matebele King Lobengula, whose country now bears your name, you dealt justly and honestly? Are these charges against you true? Say now in this the Lord's House, before your Father in Heaven as well as your father on earth and this congregation whether these evil things we hear about you are true or false.'

The congregation was deeply moved by the words of its Minister. They loved and respected him because they knew him to be a wise, generous and God-fearing man. They knew how deeply the rumours of his son's evil ways had wounded him and that he had spent long hours in his study praying for his son's soul. They were, therefore, anxious for his father's sake, that Rhodes should give his side of the story and hoped that it would be such as would restore peace and happiness to their old Vicar.

Then Rhodes, wearing his favourite white flannel trousers, blue silk tie, and loose tweed jacket, clasping the altar rails with one hand but standing erect, began to speak. His face was suntanned but showed no emotion. It was the usual unsmiling ever-serious meditating or brooding face of Rhodes, and this day it looked even more serious than ever.

'My father has said,' he began, 'that in this parish, I was taught the Christian virtues of love, purity, honesty and unselfishness. I wish to say that no one was more sensitive of and conscientious in his duty to show, both by precept and example, the teachings of Christ, than my father. Although I did not care to go to any particular church, when I became a man, because I found that if I went, for instance, up a mountain quietly, I got thoughts, what you might call

27

religious thoughts, since they were for the betterment of humanity, I knew that there was a better thing for the world than materialism, and that was religion.

'In this parish, I was also taught that while on earth, I had a duty not only to my God but also to my Queen and my Country and that I was duty bound to seize every opportunity to enlarge my Queen's Dominions. It was not always easy to reconcile one's duty to God with one's duty to Queen and Country. Since I am being accused of recklessness and greed for fame and fortune, it may be helpful if, at this stage, I give you my creed. I have been asked, "In what is your strongest belief?" I do not hesitate to reply— in power. There is the power of religion, the power of the sword, the power of philosophy, the power that drives one, what is it? If I am to believe in myself, and I do, I must have in my being the power to enable me to carry through my object. But what is the end of power? So often desert sand and ruins. But there is a force that drives one on and one cannot evade it if one would.

'I believe that we, the British, are the first race in the world and the more of the world we inhabit, the better it is for the human race. Every acre added to our territory provides for the birth of more of the British race, who otherwise would not be brought into existence. Added to which the absorption of the greater part of the world, under our rule, simply means the end of all wars.

'I believe that the English-speaking race, whether British, American, Australian or South African, is the type of race which does now and is likely to continue to do in the future, the most practical and effective work to establish justice, to promote liberty and to ensure peace over the widest possible area of this planet. Therefore, if there be a God and He cares anything about what I do, I think it is clear that He would like me to do what He is doing Himself, and as He is manifestly fashioning the English-speaking race as a chosen instrument by which He will bring in a State of Society based on justice, liberty and peace, He must obviously wish me to do what I can to give as much scope and power to the race as possible. I believe in this with all the enthusiasm bred in the soul of an inventor. It is not self-glorification I desire, but the wish to register my patent for the benefit of those who I think are the greatest people the world has seen, but whose fault is that they do not know their strength, their greatness and their destiny, and who, wasting their time on local matters had to be trained to view the world as a whole. I do not wish them to forget the Rock from which they were sprung because so long as they remember that, their success is certain, and their future assured. Many of them never realize how lucky they are to have been born Englishmen, when there are millions who are not born Englishmen!

'So, I believe it to be my duty to God, my Queen and my Country to paint the whole map of Africa red—red from Cape to Cairo. That is my creed, my dream, and my mission in life.

'I freely admit that in pursuing my object, the enlargement of the British Empire and with it the cause of peace, industry and freedom, I have adopted means of removing opposition which were the rough-and-ready way and not the highest way to attain that object; but you must remember that, in South Africa, where my work has lain, the laws of right and equity are not so fixed and established as in this country and if I have once or twice done things which savoured rather of violence than of protest or peaceful striving, you must look back to far-off times in English history for a parallel to the state of things in South Africa. In those past times, there have been not a few men who have done good service in the State, but whose actions have partaken of the violence of their time, which are hard to justify in a more law-abiding age. It is among those men that my own life and actions must be weighed, and I trust to the justice of my countrymen.

'I shall now try to show you that in my dealings with other men, and particularly the savage king of the Matebele, Lobengula, I acted in accordance with what I believed were the dictates of my duty to God, my Queen and my Country.

'Let us not forget that Lobengula's country was, at that time, considered by all European powers to be rich in gold and open to European occupation, for although the Portuguese had, in the sixteenth century, made the first contact with natives in Mashonaland, they had for a very long time done nothing more. As the 1880's drew to a close, however, they began once more to show an interest in the country by establishing, here and there, trading posts, mud ports, and persuading some chiefs to accept the Portuguese flag. They laid claim to the country ruled by Lobengula and to much of that along the banks of the Shire River.

'The Portuguese were then not the only European power interested in African possessions. The Germans also had, at this time, pegged their claim in Southern Africa by hoisting their flag at Agra Pequena on 1 May 1883 and declaring a protectorate over Damaraland and Namaqualand on 24 April 1884. I know that they were casting envious eyes over Lobengula's country because a German count called at the royal kraal and dropped some honeyed words into the royal ears. I am certain that Germany wished and hoped to claim all the country lying between the Congo and the East Coast, at that time unbounded on the west and later to be called Tanganyika.

'Although the Transvaal Republic under Paul Kruger was allowed, by the agreement to which it owed its independence, to have strictly limited relations with African tribes in the north, Kruger was, in fact, trying to establish himself there. The Boers were ever seeking new pastures and greater space; were trekking in many directions into the wilderness on so-called hunting expeditions. But the hunting was not entirely for game but for additional territory. They took their families with them and settled down on good land when they came to it and thus, in time, acquired squatter rights of settlement.

'So we had Portugal, Germany, the Transvaal and Britain, with France and Belgium sweeping down from the north, all casting envious eyes on Lobengula's country. The question was, who is going to get in first? Here is a country—an immense plateau, with an occasional belt of low country, up to the Lakes, up to the Sudan. It is so high that under the Equator it is cool. It is a country for white men and for their families. I was determined to get it. To fill it with homesteads and towns, with railways and telegraphs for the advancement of Great Britain.

'There was little point in sentimentalizing over Lobengula's position and person, no matter how much we sympathized with him, because if the British did not get in first and lay a claim to his rich country, the Portuguese, the Germans, or the Transvaal would have done so.

'As a matter of fact, it was the Transvaal's actions which compelled me to make my first open move on Matebeleland. In December 1886, Ralph Williams, who was the British agent at Pretoria, capital of the Transvaal Republic, sent me a private message to the effect that Kruger had entered into some agreement with Lobengula; that he had sent a man named Piet Grobler to Lobengula to negotiate a treaty of mutual protection between the Transvaal and Matebeleland and that Grobler had apparently succeeded in getting the signature of the king to this treaty. Ralph Williams had further stated that although it appeared that the treaty was nothing more than an exchange of friendly messages—a

31

promise of protection, a grant of the right of the Transvaal Republic to have jurisdiction over its citizens in Matebeleland and the right to establish a consulate there, the Boers were already claiming, because of this treaty, the right to mining concessions in Matebeleland. This information was confirmed by two British officers who had been in Matebeleland at that time.

'To be quite frank, I was alarmed. I did not want the Transvaal to take Matebeleland. I knew that even if they did, Germany would not have allowed the Boers to keep it, because possession of Matebeleland would have enabled Germany to stretch from Angra Pequena to Delgon Bay, and Bismarck would most certainly have found an excuse to provoke a war with the Transvaal to bring about this result. I did not wish this to happen.

'I immediately contacted Sir Sidney Shippard the Administrator of Bechuanaland, and told him my fears. He saw my point and we decided to leave immediately for Grahamstown, where Sir Hercules Robinson, the Governor and High Commissioner was spending the Christmas holiday.

'Sir Sidney arrived in Grahamstown shortly before I did, but we were together when we called on the Governor who was enjoying pony racing and other seasonal activities. I told Sir Hercules that there was no time to lose and urged him to take immediate action. I wanted us to do what we had done over our Suez Canal—annexe Bechuanaland and declare a protectorate over Matebeleland and Mashonaland, but Sir Hercules declined to do this, saying that he knew that the Colonial Office would not agree to go so far.

'Sir Hercules agreed, however, that Sir Sidney Shippard should instruct his assistant in Bechuanaland—John Moffat, whose missionary father was actually with Lobengula in Matebeleland at the time, to go to Matebeleland and ascertain the truth about the Grobler treaty and also try and get

Lobengula to sign a treaty with us, giving to Britain the sole right to influence affairs in his country. This was a great deal less than I wanted us to do, but I realized that it was all I was going to get, at the time. I decided immediately to send one of my men, Fry, to act as my agent at Lobengula's kraal. On my return to Kimberley I sent a messenger to John Moffat, with Sir Sidney's despatch, who covered the seven hundred miles to Palapye in record time, arriving there long before the end of January. I have asked John Moffat, one of the principal actors in the events that followed, to stand by and be available to tell you what happened when he met Lobengula. This, I am certain, will be so much better than anything that I, who was not in Matebeleland at the time, can tell you.'

CHAPTER FOUR

The Moffat Treaty (Tricky)

LOBENGULA'S VERSION

As someone was going outside to look for Mr John Moffat, across the seas, I saw the Royal Council of the Amandebele beginning to assemble again. I decided to go there and arrived just in time to hear the Lion uLobengula continue his testimony, saying, 'There is always a fence around the word of a king, unlike other men he cannot be a chameleon which changes every time it gets among leaves of a different colour. He must be as steady as a rock and as constant as a flowing river. I could not therefore have agreed to the words of the Boers and then immediately refused to stand by my word.'

A voice: 'Don't worry, we know that whitemen are born liars. Never trust a whiteman!'

Lobengula continued, 'It was only one moon after this visit of the Boers that uJoni [John], son of Mtshede [Rev. Robert Moffat] visited me. uJoni had come to the country to visit his father who was among us. Now, everyone here knows that there is no whiteman who stood closer to my father, the Elephant, than Joni's father. Theirs was the friendship of a cup and a waterpot. This close friendship between my father and the whiteman uMtshede, made it imperative for me to treat uJoni like my brother and accord to him the rights and privileges of princes of royal blood. This was due to him because of the love and respect we all had for my father the Bull Elephant, since he whom he had favoured with a friendship as warm and lasting as he had extended to the whiteman uMtshede, was indeed a prince among the Amandebele.

'It was because of this, that I invited uJoni to accompany me, when I reviewed 12,000 of my troops that were assembled at the royal kraal before the ceremonial slaying of the bull. As I recall, we had completed our work and were refreshing ourselves with beer when, in some way, I cannot now remember exactly how, the conversation drifted towards the various whitemen who were anxious to enter my country. I told uJoni that my majaha, a small section of whom he had just seen, were anxious and ready to bathe their spears in the blood of any whiteman who entered my country without my permission. He then asked me about the Boers and I told him that I disliked them more than any other race of whitemen because they had stolen my father's country and was certain that they would steal mine if they had the chance. I told uJoni that I did not mind the Amangisi [the English] coming because they were different, but I said that the Queen should not send too many of her people here because I did not want too many whitemen in my country. uJoni then told me that he knew of a way by which I could prevent white people from coming into my country. This way was to tell the Queen herself and she would tell the whitemen not to enter my country. Even the Boers and Amaputukezi [the Portuguese] would obey her because they all feared her. uJoni then said that in order that the Queen should believe that I had sent him, I should make a line on a piece of paper, and this line would convince the Queen that he was speaking on my behalf. I did not understand how a mere line on a piece of paper would make his Queen believe that I had sent him but if Joni believed that this line had such magic it was all right with me, so I made the line he wanted. I never heard about his piece of paper again. This did not worry me because I never believed much in the piece of paper to begin with, but if making a line on it was going to result in whitemen not pestering me for permission to enter my country, I was quite willing to try its magic.

'I, of course, did not believe all the things uJoni said about his Queen, because I knew of many people who had relied too much on the Queen and had later been eaten up by the Boers without the Queen raising a finger to help them. But I did not see anything to be gained by refusing to co-operate with Joni since he had, like a brother, volunteered to help me keep these whitemen out of my country. That is why I made the line on his paper.'

Then Mzilikazi said, 'Yes, my son, I see how your mind worked. You thought as a king and took the word of uJoni as that of a prince. Many a man is like the fruit of a fig-tree whose skin can look ripe and juicy outside when its heart is rotten inside. What would you have said, if a man had told you that uJoni had not come to the country to visit his father but had travelled all the way from Khama's country to trap you into making that line on the little piece of paper?'

'I would have doubted his word, my father, because there was nothing that uJoni or his father wanted from me except to be allowed to talk about their strange God.'

'What would you have said if another man had told you that uJoni was working for this Queen and was in league with uLodzi, the man who burnt your kraal and drove you out of your country?'

'I would have called him a liar to his face, and punished him for speaking ill of one who was like a brother to me. I

36

would never have believed it. We counted Joni, his father, and the other God-speaking men, on our side.'

'You were right, my son, in treating uJoni as a brother, because his father was my brother and that made you, our sons, brothers also, but he did not open his heart and act like a brother to you. The piece of paper you drew a line on told the world that you agreed to enter into a treaty of friendship with the Queen, as a continuation of my treaty of friendship signed with the induna of the Cape of Good Hope. It further said that you agreed that you would not discuss with, or sell or give away any part of your country to, any other white-man without first obtaining the permission of the Queen's induna.'

'That is rubbish, my father. Why should I have given away my rights like that? Why should I, a king, agree to have to ask the permission of a mere induna, an induna who allowed himself to be ruled by a woman, at that, when I want to do anything with my own country? These are shameful lies. uJoni was a miserable scoundrel indeed to lie like this.'

A voice, 'This is how he thanked you for treating him like a prince of the blood royal. Teach a dog to eat milk and the next day he will bite you.'

Another voice, 'I wish I had known all this, I would have squeezed the life out of that dog's throat with my bare hands, and thrown his carcase to the hyena.'

A third voice, 'These white dogs haven't got a single bone of truth in them.'

The meeting was in disorder, for members of the Council loudly protesting and violently gesticulating appeared to have been very much upset and agitated by the treachery and lies of one they had held in such esteem and given so high a place among them.

The cause of the Amandebele Royal Council's uproar, the Rev. John S. Moffat was, at that very moment, slowly and reverently walking up the aisle, to the altar of the church of Bishop's Stortford. He would soon be giving his version of the story so I made certain that I was present. John Moffat had proved an excellent emissary of Rhodes to Lobengula. He was the son of Robert Moffat a close friend of Mzilikazi and had been with his father when Mzilikazi permitted the missionaries to open a mission station at Inyati. To Lobengula he was familiarly known as 'uJoni'.

He began his tale. 'I was at Palapye when a despatch from Sir Sidney Shippard reached me and instructed me to go to Matebeleland without delay. I was to find out about a reported treaty between Lobengula and the Transvaal Republic through a man named Piet Grobler; ascertain its authenticity and terms and then try to persuade Lobengula to repudiate his treaty with Grobler if it existed, replacing it with one which declared his country to be within the British sphere of influence.

'The bearer of the despatch told me that he had been sent by Rhodes and had been instructed to ride as fast as he could because the message he was carrying was most urgent. He had consequently covered the seven hundred miles between Kimberley and Palapye in record time.

'I was able to leave immediately and saw the King Lobengula on 30 January 1888. He appeared fairly engrafted on the throne in spite of the fact that he was a usurper. It may interest you to know that Lobengula was not the rightful heir to the Matebele throne. The lawful heir was Nkulumane, but after Mzilikazi's death, there was some doubt whether Nkulumane was still alive and a delegation consisting of Lotshe, Nomandla, Magaba, Mtanyelo, Mhlaba (Mncumbata's son) was sent to Natal to look for him.

'It was a custom of the people from whose stock the Amandebele sprang, to exile, while he is still a boy, the heir to the chieftainship. This custom the forebears of the Amandebele had practised for many generations before they, the Amandebele, settled in their present country.

'The boy heir was exiled in such a way that the impression was created that his death or injury had been intended, and it was therefore extremely dangerous for him to return to his people while his father or king was still alive. The village in which the young heir was born was usually destroyed, the regiment to which he was attached disbanded and its leaders put to death. This was done in order to prevent political factions forming around the heir and tempting him to mischief during his father's reign and also to ensure that, when the heir becomes king, no one section of the nation will have undue influence over him.

'Langa had driven his heir Mangete to take refuge with another tribe until his father's death. Mangete, in turn, drove away his heir Matshobana who took refuge among the Amatshali tribe until the death of Mangete was announced and he returned to take over his chieftainship. Matshobana expelled Mzilikazi with his mother when the first king of the Amandebele was an infant and his mother sought refuge among the Amangwe tribe. When Matshobana died, the Amangwe chief sent Mzilikazi to his people to become their chief. So following this custom, Mzilikazi expelled Nkulumane, when he was only a little boy, to take refuge in Natal.

'In each of these cases, a younger brother usurped the throne before the rightful heir was found, but the usurper always fled when the expelled son appeared. This happened with Mangete as well as with Matshobana when Dwangubana was the usurper. In Mzilikazi's case it was uMvundlela who usurped the throne and then Lobengula usurped it in the place of Nkulumane. But Lobengula kept it for good.

The prestige of birthright together with the power and influence of the chief with whom the heir had been a fugitive overawed the usurper into abandoning resistance and taking flight. Nkulumane lived in Natal being known by the name of April or the Zulu name, Kandu. He worked for Sir Theophilus Shepstone, known to the Zulu people as uSomseu. Although Shepstone knew that he was a son of Mzilikazi, he had no idea he was the exiled heir to the Matebele throne. This fact Nkulumane concealed very carefully until the return of one Elijah Kambule from Matebeleland, where he had heard the particulars of Nkulumane's birth and exile as well as a description of Nkulumane. After questioning Nkulumane, Kambule exclaimed, "Why, you must be Nkulumane," whereupon Nkulumane admitted his identity for the first time.

'When the Governor of Natal was made aware of Nkulumane's identity he decided that while he would not prevent him from claiming his throne, he would not actively assist him. He recognized that in Nkulumane's mind he occupied the position of various chiefs who afforded refuge to his forefathers and so Nkulumane expected the same treatment from him, but he did not want to appear to be taking sides in the matter.

'Of the people sent, only Nomandla appears to have succeeded in seeing the Governor of Natal. Nomandla informed the Governor that he had been sent five months previously to Natal to ask for alliance and also to say that Lobengula considered himself a son of the Natal Government and that he wished for peace and goodwill and asked for the repose of unanxious slumber. He was also to say that Lobengula's general health was not good and so he wished the Natal Government to send him a doctor from the Amabaca tribe and with the doctor a supply of water from the Great River, the sea.

'The envoy went on to say that after the death of Mzili-kazi, his successor Nkulumane was said to have been killed by the king but that nevertheless a delegation had been sent to search for him in all directions—that the king's first son uMangwana had disappeared soon after the death of his father and that by his disappearance the Matebele had lost the person whose duty it was to advise and guide them.

'The envoy then said that he had met uMangwana that morning in the city of Pietermaritzburg for the first time since the death of his father and had conversed with him and learnt from him that Nkulumane, the real heir to the Mate-bele throne, was here and that the two brothers uMangwana and Nkulumane had recognized each other, had compared various points in their history and were satisfied each of the other's identity.

'The Governor then told Nomandla that he was always ready to receive and reciprocate friendly greetings and assur-ances from any quarter and that it was his wish to maintain peace and goodwill, not only among his own subjects, but also among his friends outside. But as regards the doctor and sea water, the Governor said that Nomandla could himself see that, under the present circumstances of the Matebele succession, complying with his request could very easily and most probably be construed as furnishing a doctor to anoint and establish the new King Lobengula and give him medi-cine to strengthen him against all claimants to the chieftain-ship.

'To this Nomandla replied that it might be so if Loben-gula belonged to a separate house from Nkulumane but he was Nkulumane's junior in the same house, and could only succeed to power in the event of Nkulumane's death—that no one knew this better than Lobengula himself and that no one had been more anxious than he that Nkulumane should be found—that he had begged to be allowed to go and search for him himself but that he had been prevented because he was the only son of the Royal House; and that should he be lost also, the line would be extinct; that it was only after two years of fruitless search that he consented to administer the Government until it should be ascertained beyond doubt that Nkulumane no longer lived; he was told to hold the nation in his hand, not that it was his, but if Nkulumane were dead, it would belong to him of right— therefore no dispute about succession could arise.

'A Zulu chief, uMantele, who was present then said, "How can you answer for what is in the heart of another?"

'To which remark Nomandla replied, "You are right, it is sweet to govern!"

'Nomandla also said that there was a party of Matebele who had arrived in Natal with uMangwana. This party, the envoy claimed, had not been officially sent by anyone who had authority to send them and had fallen out with uMangwana on the way; he had come with them but they belonged to the Zwangendaba portion of the Matebele who had refused to recognize the temporary appointment of Lobengula. They had incurred his displeasure because their refusal inferentially charged Lobengula with a desire to usurp the power of his absent brother, whereas the arrangement was a national one for the sake of meeting the requirements of the people until the main question could be placed beyond doubt—he said that it would not be proper for Nkulumane to go to his people in such company, that the fact of his existence must first be reported to the nation and the nation must send for him in a fitting and becoming manner and acknowledge the benefit that had been conferred on them by the preservation of their most important member. At this interview, Nomandla was accompanied by a man who gave his name as Adonis Murimu,

42

a member of a tribe on the Limpopo River, who had been captured by Mzilikazi's army while yet a boy and brought up to manhood at the Matebele Royal Residence in the capacity of a confidential servant and who, since then, had been to many places in the Cape and Natal colonies as servant to Boer masters and afterwards had been engaged by Boer hunters in Matebeleland. On one of these trips he had taken the opportunity to pay a visit of condolence to the Royal family, after the death of Mzilikazi. Lobengula had immediately engaged him, since he knew the country, to go to the Governor of Natal with Nomandla, who is the hereditary envoy of the king as his father was before him. Murimu confirmed what Nomandla had said but also said that since Lobengula had been appointed king already, he thought that any attempt to introduce another would be resisted and cause bloodshed. "I say this from what I see, but I belong to another tribe and cannot speak with confidence," he added.

'Nomandla quickly told him, "You are a foreigner and are not capable of offering an opinion on such a point, the feeling of the people towards hereditary right is stronger than most feelings but whether it is true that to govern is pleasant one cannot tell; it is a point for the Matebele themselves to settle when they know the truth."

'On the basis of these interviews the Governor of Natal wrote to Lobengula informing him of the existence of a claimant to his throne, and indicating that he did not wish to be involved in the dispute.

'Nkulumane was kept well informed about events in Matebeleland. When Lobengula became king, Nkulumane went to Macheng, a chief of the Bamangwato and asked for support to recover his throne. Macheng made promises and even went as far as mobilizing his forces, but did not take any action. Nkulumane died in Bechuanaland at a place called Pukeng among survivors of the Zwangendaba tribe

43

who had escaped into that country after the death of Mbiko in a clash with Lobengula. On their return the people who were sent to ascertain the whereabouts of Nkulumane either lied to Lobengula saying that they could not find Nkulumane or, if he knew the truth, it was proclaimed that the rightful heir was dead, with the object of pacifying the nation or confirming Lobengula as king. Subsequently, the truth must have leaked out for Mhlaba was executed by Lobengula, "for having deceived the king". Mnyenyezi, another son of Mncumbata and Nteveve, Mhlaba's son, fled the country and later guided the British South African Police column into Matebeleland.

'Anyway, Lobengula received me very cordially and spoke of the friendship of our fathers. He asked me to be with him as he reviewed his troops before the ceremonial slaying of the bull.

'After this ceremony, I asked him about the Grobler Treaty and he denied that he had invited the Boers to enter the country, saying quite plainly that he detested them because they had stolen his father's land and wanted to steal his also. When I spoke about the dangers of European nations entering his country and told him of the benevolence and power of the Queen, he readily agreed to sign a treaty which I had drawn up as follows:

The Chief Lobengula, Ruler of the tribe known as the Amandebele, together with the Mashona and Makalaka tributaries of the same, hereby agrees to the following articles and conditions.

That peace and amity shall continue for ever between Her Britannic Majesty, her subjects and the Amandebele people; and the contracting Chief Lobengula engages to use his utmost endeavours to prevent any rupture of the same, to cause the strict observance of his treaty, and so

44

to carry out the treaty of friendship which was entered into by his late father, the Chief Mzilikazi, with the then Governor of the Cape of Good Hope, in the year of Our Lord 1836.

It is hereby further agreed by Lobengula, Chief in and over the Amandebele country, with the dependencies as aforesaid, on behalf of himself and people, that he will refrain from entering into any correspondence or treaty with any foreign state or power to sell, alienate or cede or permit or countenance any sale, alienation or cession of the whole or any part of the said Amandebele country under his chieftainship, or upon any other subject without the previous knowledge and sanction of Her Majesty's High Commissioner for South Africa ...

In faith of which I, Lobengula, on my part have hereto set my hand at Gubulawayo, Amandebeleland, this 11th day of February, and of Her Majesty's reign the 51st.

> Lobengula, his X mark
> Witnesses: W. Graham
> S. B. Van Wyk
> Before me, J. S. Moffat
> Assistant
> Commissioner

Although I could understand Sindebele fairly well, I took with me one who was considered an expert in the language —the Rev. C. D. Helm—who acted as an interpreter, and Messrs. W. Graham and S. B. Van Wyk witnessed the treaty.'

The Rev. Rhodes then said, 'Mr. Moffat, I am sure you will not mind answering a few questions.'

'No, I won't mind. Please go ahead and ask.'

'You will also not mind, if for a moment, I forget that I am an Englishman and scrutinize your actions to determine

45

whether they were in accordance with the teaching of Christ, because that is our prime object here.

'Did Lobengula know that you were in fact a servant of the Queen and you had gone to Matebeleland for the specific purpose of signing a treaty with him?'

'I do not think so. No, I do not think he knew that.'

'And why did you not let him know that?'

'Well, quite frankly, I would not have been able to get his signature to my treaty. You see, the mind of a native like Lobengula works in a most curious manner. If I had let him know that he had something valuable or important that I wanted, then his attitude towards me would have been very different. He would not have been friendly and what took me a day to accomplish might have taken me several weeks or months while he hesitated and consulted every one of his indunas.'

'Did you sign this treaty on behalf of the Queen?'

'Good heavens, no! I had no authority to do that and you will notice that nowhere in the treaty do I say that I represent the Queen. I merely witnessed Lobengula's signature as a Government official.'

'Would, therefore, a treaty—a contract—in which there was only one contracting party instead of at least two, be legal, do you think?'

'It would most likely not be able to stand in court but don't forget that there were hundreds of such treaties being made all over Africa and on their basis the continent was being carved up. I think the treaty was acceptable, internationally, in fact, I know that it was; the Transvaal, Germany and Portugal all gave up their claims to Matebeleland because of this treaty.'

'So Britain was able to ward off and dispose of her rivals in Matebeleland by using this treaty. This is the benefit you sought that she should derive from the treaty, is it not?'

'Yes, it is.'

'What benefit did Lobengula and the Matebele derive from it?'

'Well, Lobengula and his indunas who were becoming more and more apprehensive of the increasing influx of white men into their country, for animal as well as mineral hunting, were able to say that they had already come to some arrangement with the British.'

'You mean that the British were able to say that for them?'

'Yes, I believe that is more correct.'

'Did that decrease the number of white men seeking to enter the country?'

'No, it did not. But although the numbers did not decrease the national rivalry as between the Boers and Portuguese, for instance, was eliminated.'

'So, from this treaty the Matebele only benefited by the elimination of the Boers, Portuguese, and Germans as rivals of the British for influence in their country.'

'Yes.'

'Would it not be fairer to say the British benefited more by this treaty since their rivals were removed from the scene?'

'Yes, it would.'

'Do you think, then, that for the benefit of removing Britain's rivals from the scene, a king such as Lobengula would willingly give up his power as king, to sell, alienate or cede his country and bind himself to doing this only with the knowledge and sanction of the British High Commissioner for South Africa?'

'I am bound to say that the bargain appears to be too much in favour of Britain.'

'You agree that no envoy would have thought of propounding such a proposition to any monarch in Europe?'

'I agree.'

'You agree that you did not commit Britain even to keeping the peace with Lobengula, let alone defending him if he were attacked?'

'I do.'

'Yet if you led Lobengula to believe anything, it was that the Queen was his ally.'

'In a general sort of a way—yes.'

'So you were able to get Lobengula's signature to this treaty because he trusted you as a brother and because he could neither read nor understand all the things you had written.'

'That is so.'

'Is it not fair to conclude, therefore, that this treaty was just as fraudulent and as bogus as you and your friends claimed the Boer Grobler's had been fraudulent?'

'I do not enjoy saying it, but I have to admit that it was.'

'Is it not disgraceful that you, not only a minister's son, but also a minister of the Gospel yourself, should have been involved in perpetrating such a fraud?'

'It depends on how you look at it. I can only say that I was doing my duty to my Queen and Country and carrying out instructions, as a civil servant.'

'Did you not mind doing this duty and carrying out these instructions even if they led you to doing what you must have known to be basically dishonest and fraudulent?'

'I did mind. I was fighting my conscience all the time. I knew old Lobengula never really understood what I committed him to and even if he had understood, I knew that he had given away a lot, and had received practically nothing in return. I hated that I should have been the one to pull this fast one on him, especially since I could only have done it by prostituting the position and status which Matebele etiquette generously accorded me because of my father's friendship with Mzilikazi. But I was a diplomat in the service of my

48

Queen and wanted to succeed on missions I was sent. Furthermore, I believed that the Matebele state was evil and had caused a great deal of sorrow, misery and death throughout the land. Think of the women and children whom the Matebele methods of war had killed like flies. I believed that it was God's wish that this system should be changed and the land rid of the power of the Matebele.

'I also honestly believed that the British people would, more than anyone else, be able to bring about peace, good government, and civilization to the people over whom Lobengula had such unjust sway. If we had not moved in, others would have, and the natives might have been worse off. I am, therefore, not ashamed of the part I played in breaking down Lobengula's power, even though what I did may have been fraudulent.'

The Rev. John Moffat had spoken with such great feeling and deep conviction that this won him the respect of many in the congregation even though they were convinced that his actions had been unworthy of, particularly, a minister of the Gospel; and his treaty fraudulent and bogus.

Cecil Rhodes now, again, took the stand at the altar rails.

CHAPTER FIVE

The Rudd Concession

'As I have already said,' Rhodes began, 'anticipating the success of Moffat's mission to Lobengula, I arranged, before I left Grahamstown, for one of my men, Fry, to represent me at Lobengula's kraal. I did not know that Fry was, in fact, a sick man suffering from cancer. It was not long, therefore, before he was back in Kimberley and died soon after.

'His death thus left me without an agent in Matebeleland. For several reasons, I considered this vacuum to be most unsatisfactory and detrimental to British interests in the country. For one, I wanted to be kept informed of what was going on at Lobengula's kraal because I knew that even though Moffat had Lobengula's signature on his treaty, there was a chance of the old buster being persuaded by our rivals —the Boers, the Germans or the Portuguese—to change his mind about the British and repudiate the treaty altogether. For another, I wanted to take the first chance and move in before representatives of other British interests had a foothold in the country, for fortune favours him who takes the first chance and luck is only a question of getting up early. And lastly, I knew that nature abhors a vacuum and that sooner or later the vacuum at the king's kraal would be filled. I was determined to be the one to fill it. Since I could not, myself, go to Matebeleland, I chose three men to represent me there. They were Rudd, Thompson and Maguire.

'I could rely on Charles Rudd to look after the business side of things. He had been my partner, in business, from the early days I set up camp in Kimberley, and although he was not the adventurous or imaginative type always yearning for new conquests and ready to risk everything to make more, I knew him to be a sound businessman, completely loyal to me and absolutely reliable. F. R. Thompson, who was popularly known as "Matebele Thompson" was an expert in native affairs. Not only could he speak a number of native languages fluently but he could also understand the native mind and how it works better than any white man I knew. He had been my secretary in Bechuanaland before I put him in charge of the De Beers native compounds with the special responsibility of preventing the illicit sale of diamonds. He had the advantage of having been to Bulawayo before and of having been known to the king who, it was believed, had taken a liking to him. Thompson had one unfortunate weakness, however, and that was, as a boy he had seen natives murder his father by the unusual method of forcing a ramrod down his throat through to the back. No man was ever likely to forget such an experience and as will be seen later, this made him apt to crack and lose his nerve at a critical moment when under pressure. He was, in spite of this, the best person on whom I could place the responsibility of directly dealing with Lobengula—humouring him, lobbying for support among the indunas and making certain that generally no member of the group fouled the nest by ignorantly treading on Matebele susceptibilities and violating their myriad of customs.

'Rochfort Maguire was a lawyer by profession. He had been a student at Oxford when I was there and had gained a double first and a Fellowship of All Souls. He was as learned and erudite as he was cultured. Small of stature, meticulous and always immaculately dressed, he would have been more at home in academic circles or passing biscuits and tea in the elegant drawing-rooms of England than in the role of a pioneer envoy and diplomat to the fly-infested court of a savage king, that I cast him. I wanted him, however, to put in good legal language and form any agreement or concession the groups might be able to extract from Lobengula. Thus Rudd was to look after the business aspect of the transaction, Thompson to keep an eye on and deal with the natives, while Maguire saw to it that any agreement entered into was not subsequently nullified on the grounds of inexact language or inappropriate form.

'I had no difficulty in persuading Rudd and Maguire to go, but when I broached the subject to Thompson, he immediately said, "I must ask my wife."

' "I knew you would say that," I replied, as I pulled out of my pocket the written consent his wife had given me, for I had thought it prudent to secure her permission before asking him to go on this mission to Matebeleland.'

'What exactly did you want? Was it more gold or diamonds?' his father, the Rev. Rhodes, asked.

'I am grateful for the opportunity to clarify that point, because there have been many suggestions made about what I really wanted. I wanted one thing and one thing alone, and that was to extend the Cape Colony into Central Africa by creating a new country where men and women of British stock would settle permanently in peace and prosperity for the glory of their motherland. That was the one and only aim of my endeavours. It has been suggested that I was, above all, interested in gold and diamonds. This is not absolutely true. The discovery of diamonds in Matebeleland at this time, would, in fact, have been harmful to my personal interests since it would have affected the price of diamonds in South Africa. I was, of course, interested in minerals—gold or diamonds—but not for the sole purpose of increasing my wealth.

'I realized that in order to create a country such as I had in mind, it was necessary to have money for the occupation and development of the new territory. I knew that, at that time, the British Government was not prepared, under any circumstances, to listen to any schemes for territorial expansion which involved them in spending money. I also knew human beings well enough to realize the futility of appealing for such funds on purely philanthropic grounds, for pure philanthropy is all very well in its way but philanthropy plus five per cent is a good deal better. So, it was only in so far as the prospect of the discovery of gold in Matebeleland enabled me to have reasonable grounds for offering the five per cent on philanthropy that I was interested in minerals. But for the belief that the country was rich in gold I would not have been able to persuade anyone to invest money in Matebeleland. So I had before all else to secure a concession giving me the sole right to all minerals from Lobengula; with the concession in my hand I would then ask the British Government for a charter such as had been granted to the British East India Company. I knew that they were unlikely to reject my request if I had a concession in my hand. That was the purpose of the mission I was sending to Matebeleland. I, of course, did not intend that Lobengula should, at that time, know exactly what I was up to—planning the seizure of his country by hook or by crook, although I suspected that he had a pretty good idea of what was going to happen. I frankly admit, therefore, that even as early as when I sent Rudd, Thompson and Maguire to negotiate a mineral concession with Lobengula, I had long before decided to dispossess him of his land and the only pertinent question was how. Prudence dictated that I should do it one step at a time and not show my hand until the last minute. This is what I tried to do.

'I shall now ask Rudd, Thompson and Maguire to come forward and tell you of their journey to Lobengula's kraal and what took place there.' All eyes turned to the three men who were in the congregation, as they stood up and walked to the altar. The tall bearded Charles Rudd spoke first. 'We left Kimberley at the end of August 1888, with a letter of introduction from Sir Hercules Robinson, the British High Commissioner and Governor of the Cape of Good Hope, to Lobengula. The letter merely stated that we were highly respectable gentlemen visiting his country. My son Frank and his friend Denny decided to join us. We reached Bulawayo on 20 September 1888 and found a number of white men already there. They were the missionaries Helm and Mackenzie, the well-known traders Sam Edwards of Tati, Usher and Fairbairn, who kept Lobengula's seal which appeared on all the king's documents. There was the syndicate of Wood, Francis, and Chapman; Boggie, Chadwick and Wilson; Rennie-Taylor, Boyle, and Riley, who represented Mr Edward A. Lippert and a group of German banks, and A. E. Maund, who was representing Lord Gifford and Mr George Cawston of the Exploiting and Exploring Company. There were others . . .' (and here Thompson chipped in and said, 'The Foreign Legion—a band of needy adventurers who prowled about the royal kraal like human jackals'), 'and,' Rudd continued, 'Dr Knight Bruce, the Anglican Bishop of Bloemfontein who was seeking permission to open a mission station in Mashonaland. Through the good offices of John Moffat we were without delay given an audience by Lobengula. At a respectable distance we removed our hats and courteously approached, shook hands with him, and presented him with a greeting gift of a hundred sovereigns.

'I found Lobengula just what I expected him to be—a

very fine man, only very fat, but with a beautiful skin and well proportioned. He had a curious face which looked partly worried, partly good-natured and partly cruel. He had, however, a very pleasant smile.

'The Rev. C. D. Helm of the London Missionary Society interpreted for us. We were generously served with food—masses of half-cooked meat, enough to feed an army, which we had to tear into pieces with our bare hands, and, of course, drank large quantities of beer.

'The king listened to our plea for a mineral concession with divided attention. He constantly left us for some thirty minutes at a time, to mix medicines for the rain to fall in the country. He appeared, however, to pay more attention and to listen more attentively and sympathetically when Helm offered his personal advice to him, which was that Lobengula's wisest plan was to make friends with only one group—the group that was the strongest, and send everyone else away empty-handed. The Rev. Helm, of course, hinted that we were the strongest group. Lobengula's trusted senior induna Lotshe also gave advice in our favour.' Here Thompson again broke in, saying, 'What Lobengula, of course, did not know was that we had fixed both his advisers. The Rev. Helm had, in fact, accepted a bribe and was working for Rhodes. I had made a secret agreement with Lotshe whereby he had agreed to receive three hundred gold sovereigns, if he successfully helped us to win the concession.'

Rudd continued, 'We made the offer, but at this point Lobengula heard that Sir Sidney Shippard, the Deputy High Commissioner was not very far from his border and wanted to visit him. He therefore decided not to come to any firm decision before hearing what Sir Sidney had to say.'

And for the first time the dapper Maguire contributed to the narrative, saying, 'Yes, and so we waited and waited and waited. We went to hunt for game, bathed in the river, played whist, backgammon or chess until we were worn out. The food was awful and made me sick. Old Rudd here could take it no more. He decided to quit and asked the king for the road, but fortunately for him, the old blighter refused to let him go. It was during this time that one day I went to bathe in a pool along a stream that was near by. I had taken off my shoes and trousers but fortunately still wore my shirt, when I decided to clean my teeth, using a toothpaste that coloured the water in the pool. In the calm peace and quiet of the African forest that summer day, my thoughts were in far-off England as I gazed at the ripples of coloured water extending outwards and outwards, growing larger and larger in successive rings, until they lost both their colour and momentum in the staid and deeper regions of the sullen pool. I was thus lost in meditation when a savage battle-cry tore the air, and in a twinkle of an eye, four hideous-looking Matebele warriors had seized my arms and legs, and a fifth was threatening to thrust his spear into my body. I have never been more frightened in my life. I thought that the day of my exit from this earth had arrived and closed my eyes, expecting to feel, any moment, the sharp point of a Matebele spear piercing through to my heart. No spear cut my flesh. I opened my eyes, trembling with fear and wet with sweat. I was dragged to the royal kraal and charged before the king with bewitching the river and making it run red. Thanks to the eloquence and persuasive powers of the induna Lotshe, I was released.' 'And,' added Thompson, 'he never took a bath again until he left Matebeleland. Pity the warriors didn't find him naked. The Matebele would have seen their money's worth.'

Maguire continued, 'But the persuasive powers of Lotshe might well have been unsuccessful if the king had not been expecting the arrival of Sir Sidney Shippard who, Lobengula's spies had reported, was a magician, because he had, like myself, been seen taking a bath in the river. This actually led to Sir Sidney being delayed for some time at the border, since Lobengula could not readily permit someone he knew to be a magician to enter the country lest he should practise his magic on him. Lobengula's spies also told him that Sir Sidney had an army of fifteen men—the vanguard of a large army that was coming to attack the Matebele. The king therefore knew that punishing or executing me for witchcraft would oblige him to mete out the same punishment to Sir Sidney who had been accused of the same thing. He also knew that such executions would most certainly have resulted in war with the British, and this he was not prepared to risk at the time.

'Sir Sidney arrived on 16 October 1888, with an escort of fifteen troopers. Matebele soldiers hurled insults at them and begged for the opportunity to eat them up. But fortunately, not understanding the language the troopers thought the Matebele were singing praises to them and smiled back. The Matebele appear to have been tremendously impressed by the dignified little pot-bellied figure of Sir Sidney, in tightly buttoned black frock-coat, on which was pinned the glittering star of the Order of St. Michael and St. George, grey kid gloves and patent-leather boots; on his bald head Sir Sidney wore a large white solar topee and in his hand carried a malacca cane with an ornate silver knob. Accompanying him were his A.D.C., Major Goold-Adams, Moffat, Helm and Dr Knight Bruce. Lobengula was obviously impressed and delighted. He ordered chairs to be placed for his guests in the shade of the historic indaba tree and behaved with obvious propriety throughout Sir Sidney's audience with him. Perhaps Sir Sidney would not mind telling us what took place at this indaba with the Matebele king.'

The little pot-bellied Sir Sidney rose and walked towards

the altar rails. He still had his famous Dundreary whiskers, and although he was not wearing his tightly buttoned black frock-coat, he still managed to look impressive and dignified. He began, 'There isn't much to say about my conversation with Lobengula on 16 October 1888; I had been in Bechuanaland investigating certain allegations concerning the circumstances attending the death of a man called Piet Grobler when, realizing that I was so close to Matebeleland, I decided to make a courtesy call on Lobengula. I had, therefore, nothing special I wanted to tell him. But the subject of a concession for minerals came up and I told Lobengula that Her Majesty's Government did not wish to be involved in the matter and was not associated with any of the groups then begging for a concession. Lobengula asked me, however, whether I knew Rhodes and whether he was one of the children of the Great White Queen. In reply I told the king that I knew Rhodes very well and that he was an Englishman and as such, was indeed one of the queen's children. He appeared to be satisfied by my reply and did not raise the matter again. I also advised him to select one strong group and deal with that group alone. We then discussed affairs in his country, and I got the impression that Lobengula and some of his most intimate advisers among the great indunas were delighted, literally overjoyed at the prospect of an English alliance, since they had found out that we were not going to make any exorbitant demands as a price. Lobengula's position, I thought, was most difficult and precarious. He had to consult all the great indunas on all public questions affecting the whole country and the dominant Matebele race. He had to consider the feelings and wishes of the "indudlas"—the married warriors entitled to wear the Zulu headring—who formed the second line of defence, he had to stave off, by all possible means, the threatened rebellion of the "majahas"—whose insatiable vanity and almost incredible conceit led them to believe themselves to be invincible. He had to deal with a steadily increasing influx of European concession hunters who were becoming a source of serious anxiety to him and whom he was finding it more and more difficult to protect from the bloodthirsty "majahas". A majaha rebellion, an attempted revolution, and civil war appeared to me not unlikely. And lastly, he had a perpetual dread of an inroad of Boers from the Zoutpansberg. He knew all about Majuba and the retrocession of the Transvaal. He knew how England, after the fairest of promises, had handed over 750,000 unwilling natives to the Boers, whom they dreaded and detested. Lobengula was sharp enough and far-sighted enough to understand that the English alliance was his best card if only he could trust the English, but there was the rub. England had a bad name in South Africa for breaking faith with natives.

'I did the best I could to reassure him on this point. I told him that Her Majesty was willing to send a permanent representative to live among his people if and when he was ready to receive one. He appeared to believe my words.

'Some time after that, I left Matebeleland for Kimberley. A few days later, I was overtaken on the road by Rudd, who was travelling very light. Rudd informed me that soon after my departure, the king had summoned them to his kraal and readily signed a concession in favour of Rhodes. I was surprised by this sudden turn of events as I had seen no indication that the king was anywhere near taking a decision on the matter. On my arrival at Kimberley, I, of course, made an official report to the High Commissioner at the Cape.'

As the little, pot-bellied knight walked back to resume his seat among the congregation, Rudd took up the tale once more. 'Yes, on 28 October 1888, the king summoned us to the royal kraal. We found him sitting on an empty wooden box in a corner of the buck kraal. Although he appeared anxious, he was in good spirits. For the next two days we argued and reasoned with him and his council. I harped on the theme that if the Matebele did not have the friends and rifles we offered, more powerful enemies like the Boers and Portuguese could invade their country and wipe them out. But if they had friends like the Queen and guns, they would not only be able to call on their friends for help but would also be able to defend themselves with their rifles. Lotshe, the king's most trusted induna, and Helm took the same line of argument and supported us very strongly. At last Lobengula relented and said that he would sign our concession. We were overjoyed but did not show our feelings lest this should make him change his mind. At midday on 30 October 1888 Lobengula made his mark on the document. The Rev. C. D. Helm witnessed it and also signed an interpreter's certificate testifying that the concession had been fully interpreted and explained by himself to the Chief Lobengula and his full council of indunas and that all the constitutional usages of the Matebele nation had been complied with prior to his executing the same.

'This is the complete text of the concession that was signed by Lobengula:

Know all men by these presents, that whereas Charles Dunnell Rudd, of Kimberley; Rochfort Maguire, of London; and Francis Robert Thompson, of Kimberley, hereinafter called grantees, have covenanted and agreed, and do hereby covenant and agree to pay me, my heirs, and successors, the sum of one hundred pounds sterling, British currency, on the first day of every lunar month and further, to deliver at my Royal Kraal one thousand Martini Henri rifles, together with one hundred thousand rounds of suitable ball cartridge, five hundred of the said rifles and fifty thousand of the said cartridges to be ordered from England forthwith, and delivered as soon as the said grantees shall have commenced to work mining machinery within my territory, and further, to deliver on the Zambezi River, a steamboat with guns suitable for defence purposes upon the said river, or in lieu of the said steamboat, should I so elect, to pay to me the sum of five hundred pounds sterling, British currency, on the execution of these presents. I, Lobengula, king of Matebeleland, Mashonaland, and other adjoining territories, in the exercise of my sovereign powers, and in the presence and with the consent of my Council of indunas, do hereby grant and assign unto the said grantees, their heirs, representatives, and assigns, jointly and severally, the complete and exclusive charge over all metals and minerals situated and contained in my kingdom, principalities and dominions, together with full power to do all things that they may deem necessary to win and procure the same, and to hold, collect, and enjoy the profits and revenues, if any, derivable from the said metals and minerals, subject to the aforesaid payment. And whereas I have been much molested of late by divers persons seeking and desiring to obtain grants and concessions of land and mining rights in my territories, I do hereby authorize the said grantees, their heirs, representatives, and assigns to take all necessary and lawful steps to exclude from my kingdom, principalities, and dominions, all persons seeking land, metals, minerals, or mining rights therein; and I do hereby undertake to render them such needful assistance as they may from time to time require for the exclusion of such persons, and to grant no concessions of land or mining rights from and after this date without their consent and concurrence, provided that if at any time the said monthly payment of one hundred pounds shall be in arrear for a period of three months then this grant shall cease and determine from the date of the last made payment; and, further, provided that nothing contained in these presents shall extend to or affect a grant made by me of certain mining rights in a portion of my territory south of the Rama Kaban River, which grant is commonly known as the Tati Concession. This, given my hand this thirtieth day of October in the year of our Lord, eighteen hundred and eighty-eight, at my Royal Kraal.

Signed Lobengula   His

X

Mark

Witnesses: Signed C. D. Rudd

Signed C. D. Helm   Rochfort Maguire

J. G. Dreyer   F. R. Thompson

'Furthermore, the Rev. C. D. Helm made the following endorsement on the original agreement signed:

I hereby certify that the accompanying document has been fully interpreted and explained by me to the Chief Lobengula and his full council of indunas and that all the constitutional usages of the Matebele nation have been complied with prior to his executing the same.

Dated at Umgusa River this thirtieth day of October 1888.

Signed: Chas. D. Helm

At this point, the Rev. Rhodes interrupted the narrative and asked, 'Do you mean to say, Mr. Rudd, that you gave the impression to Lobengula that by signing your concession he was entering into some kind of a treaty in which he could call on the Queen if he were attacked by Boers or Portuguese?'

'Yes, sir, we gave just that impression.'

'But was that a correct impression?'

'In theory, no. We had no power to commit the Queen like that, but in practice, yes. If, for instance, the Boers had tried to interfere in any way with Lobengula, the British Government would for different reasons not have allowed them. This is the point we made.'

'I see! You meant that Britain would, for her own selfish ends, let us say, not allow the Matebele to be molested, because in actual fact she was only waiting for an appropriate opportunity to molest them herself?'

'That is correct.'

'You did not, of course, commit Britain to not molesting Lobengula.'

'No, we did not.'

'And, naturally, you did not make this clear to Lobengula. As a matter of fact, you deliberately created the opposite impression in his mind. You made it appear to him that implicit in this treaty was the fact that the British would not attack him, did you not?'

'Yes, we did. I made him take that for granted.'

'And yet, as a matter of fact, with Britain's connivance, only a few years later you attacked Lobengula and took his country. Is that not correct?'

'Yes, that is correct.'

'Was that not a dishonest and dirty thing for Christian men to do?'

'I am afraid it was, but then, I never professed to care very much for Christianity, nor indeed do I believe that most Englishmen do, except in such matters as being christened, married and buried.'

'I see. Is the Rev. Helm here?'

Thompson answered, 'Yes, he is here.'

'Will he come forward, please?'

A reverend gentleman in clerical collar stepped forward to the altar rails.

'Are you the Rev. Charles D. Helm, a minister ordained by the London Missionary Society?'

'Yes, sir, I am.'

'Is it true that during the time you served as an interpreter at Lobengula's court, you were secretly in the employ of my son, Cecil Rhodes?'

'It is.'

'Did you tell Lobengula this?'

'No, I did not.'

'Why?'

'I did not see anything to be gained by telling him.'

'Is it true that Lobengula took pains to pay particular attention to your advice on the subject of a mineral concession in his country?'

'It is true, he did.'

'Is it not true that he listened to your advice so attentively because he believed you to be impartial in the matter?'

'I think he did.'

'Why then did you not, in all honesty let him know that the impartiality he was ascribing to you was misplaced?'

'Because there was nothing to be gained by doing that and furthermore, my views were not necessarily coloured by the fact that I was employed by your son.'

'But you were not free to express any other views but those of your employer.'

'That may be so. But it also just happened that my employer's views were also my views. So I honestly expressed them.'

'Don't you think, then, that in appearing to be impartial when you were not, you were in fact, dishonest?'

'No, I do not. I never told Lobengula that I was impartial. If he ascribed impartiality to me that was his own business.'

'But you knew him to be doing this and permitted him to do so.'

'Yes, I did, because there was nothing to be gained by telling him otherwise.'

'You keep on saying this as if your morality is based on gain?'

'No. It is not. It is based on prudence and that means doing what is right and, if people ascribe to me motives that I do not have (such as, for instance, that I am a minister of the Gospel because I thought it was an easy life), ignoring them and continue to do what is right.'

'And what was right in this case?'

'What was right in this case was that the Matebele power should be broken completely. I believed this to be the will of God. We laboured for more than twelve years before we baptized our first convert to the Christian faith in Matebeleland. This was due to the fear of Mzilikazi and his son Lobengula. Since their regime stood between men and God it was necessary for the regime to be removed.'

'And you did not care how the regime was removed?'

'I cared. I would not have had them murdered, for instance, but I was quite prepared to let them walk into a trap that would eventually remove them from the scene.'

'So you explained the concession in a manner that made them walk into the trap.'

'I put such an interpretation on the concession as they were capable of understanding. After all, I did not fully understand the document myself.'

'And since you wanted Lobengula to sign the concession —your interpretation was a favourable one.'

'Yes, it was.'

'You did not, for instance, tell them that the document in

65

no way committed Britain to defending them in case of attack by say, Khama?'

'I did not.'

'You did not tell them that Britain herself was left free to attack them whereas they were required to keep the peace.'

'I did not.'

'You did not draw their attention to the fact that the phrase "together with full power to do all things that they may deem necessary to win and procure same", could be construed in a manner disadvantageous to them?'

'I did not.'

'So you told them only what you wanted them to know, although they thought you were telling them everything. Since you wanted their power broken, even by being led into a trap, what you, in fact, told them was such as led them to the signing of the concession, which just happened to coincide with the wishes of those who paid you to do just that.'

'Yes.'

'A remarkable story. An even more remarkable missionary.'

Rudd continued: 'By 4 p.m. that day, I was on the road to Kimberley with the valuable concession in my pocket. I did not wish to remain one minute longer in Matebeleland in case the king changed his mind and withdrew his signature. I left Thompson and Maguire to hold the fort at the king's kraal. But I almost did not make it to Kimberley. In the desert, I rode away from my son Frank and his friend Denny. I lost my way and could not retrace my steps to them. I shouted, whistled and did all sorts of things to attract their attention, without success. The heat was oppressive with the temperature at 112 degrees in the shade. I had no water with me, although my saddlebags had a few bottles of champagne, brandy and stout. I rode on and on

66

to I knew not where, for what seemed eternity, in the glare and heat of that desert sun. Eventually, almost completely incapacitated by extreme exhaustion, heat, hunger and thirst, I dropped the concession and gold I had on me in an ant-bear hole and with great difficulty wrote what I had done on a piece of paper, stuck it to a tree and remounted my horse. The horse stumbled and fell, hurting me so much that I could not stand up. But as I lay almost delirious with pain, heat, thirst and exhaustion, a bushman found me and restored my strength with water. He took me to the nearest village, where the natives nursed me with such kindness and concern as I shall never forget, until I was strong enough to retrieve the concession and gold and make my way to Kimberley, where needless to say, Rhodes was most delighted with the news of our success in Matebeleland.'

CHAPTER SIX

The Rudd Deception

When the Royal Council of the Amandebele had calmed down again, the Lion uLobengula continued his narrative.

'uJoni left our land and returned to his home in Khama's country. Several moons passed before he came back again. When he came, however, he brought three other whitemen, one of whom I recognized as uTomusoni [Thompson] for he had been in our country before. The other men, uLadi [Rudd] and uMaguire, none of us had seen before.

'These men brought a letter which uMfundisi Helm said was written by the Queen's induna at the Cape and informed me that these three men were well known and respectable men.

'These men then told me that they had been sent by another man called uLodzi [Rhodes] who was a big man in the Cape. uLodzi wanted them to get from me permission to dig a hole for gold in my country and offered to give me some of the gold they found. I asked them why uLodzi had not, himself, come to see me and they replied that he would have come but was very busy at the time, so he had sent them to be his mouth, eyes, and ears.

'I did not say anything to them then. But in their absence I asked the advice of my senior induna uLotshe. Lotshe advised me to think over the matter carefully because he believed these men to be different from the other whitemen who were at my kraal. Lotshe also said that these men had the bearing of indunas and men of high birth. I therefore allowed them to see me again.

'On the second occasion they saw me, uLadi said that the Amandebele had many enemies among whitemen because whitemen envied the Amandebele's country since it had more gold and diamonds than any other country in the world. Because of this, he said, the Amandebele will never be allowed to live in peace. So it was wise and necessary for the Amandebele to have good friends who would help them when they were attacked by white nations like the Boers or Amaputukezi. I was impressed by this argument. uLadi further stated that the Queen was ready to be our friend and to protect us from the armies of these other white races. He said that he was prepared, if we allowed him to dig this hole, to give us guns—one thousand rifles and a hundred thousand rounds of ammunition so that the Amandebele could defend themselves against whitemen. Remembering how a few Boers with guns had been able to kill many brave Mandebele soldiers across the Limpopo, I saw the wisdom of his words indeed. uLadi further promised to give me a boat, full of guns, which would sail along the Zambezi watching to see that enemies of the Amandebele did not come into the country from behind and attack us while we were unaware of their coming. Again, I liked what this man said and saw the wisdom of his words. The Amandebele would indeed be a strong nation if they had all these guns and a gunboat on the Zambezi. I remembered how our army had been defeated by the tribes across the Zambezi because it had operated from a base too far away. I thought that Amandebele soldiers living in a boat with guns on the Zambezi would be a constant reminder to those tribes across the river that we are always ready to defend our country.

'I was also impressed by what the uMfundisi uHelemu said. Helemu advised me to accept what these men offered because they were big men and very strong indeed. He referred to some whitemen, then at my kraal, as little men whose word did not count and who were not even known by other whitemen and spoke of the wisdom of dealing with one group that was big and strong instead of talking to a lot of little men. Helemu told me that in his opinion, uLodzi's men were the best group.

'Now, we all knew Helemu as a trustworthy man and a man of honour and integrity. We knew that he had nothing to gain in all this and indeed, he had told us that he valued more the riches that would come to him when he died than the riches of this earth. Helemu was one of us. He lived with us and understood us. Surely he would not give us bad advice. After all he feared his Mlimu who, he told us, wanted all men to be good and live in peace. Because of all this, I listened to his advice.

'Lotshe also advised me to accept the offer of Lodzi's men. At this time I did not understand why. When one of these men was caught red-handed practising magic and putting medicines in the water so that when the Amandebele drank this water they would cease to be strong and their women would bear them children no more, it was Lotshe who pleaded for the white magician's life saying that it was a custom of whitemen to bathe regularly in the river.

'It was about this time that I was told that an induna of the Queen wished to be given the road to come and see me. My soldiers also reported that this man, like Lotshe's friend, dabbled in magic. I had a good mind to refuse him the road, but uJoni, Helemu and Lotshe all said that I should let him come because he was a very big induna indeed. I agreed.

'The man came. His name, I believe, was Shippard. He carried himself like an induna, although I could not understand how such a little man could be an induna or a great warrior. It seemed to me that he would be easy to kill in battle. But I suppose a small body is not a disadvantage with whitemen because they shoot with guns and do not fight hand-to-hand as we do. Nevertheless, Shippard came and I liked talking to him. He was indeed an induna, for even the way he dressed showed this. He was also a clever man.

'I asked him about uLodzi and he said that it was true uLodzi was a big man and one of the children of the Queen. When uShippard left I sent a word to Ladi telling him to come and see me again. He came accompanied by uTomusoni, Maguire and Helemu. We again discussed the matter of this hole they wanted to dig in my country.

'I recalled that shortly before the falling of the Mountain, when uMncumbata was regent, because my father was sick, he gave permission for whitemen to dig a hole and look for gold somewhere near Tati. The digging of this hole had, so far, given us no trouble. It occurred to me, therefore, that we might safely do this again especially if we would thereby get guns and ammunition to make us as strong as whitemen.

'I told uLadi, Tomusoni, Maguire and Helemu that I had listened to their words and had heard all the things they had said. But, before I said anything about the digging of a hole for gold in my country, I wished them to go and get all the things they had said they would give me—the one thousand guns and one hundred thousand rounds of ammunition, the gunboat on the Zambezi and the money they had promised they would give me. I told them to go and get all those things first. I said that when they put them here in front of me, I would then allow them to dig their hole.

'The whitemen agreed to this and went away for some time. When they returned they had a piece of paper which they handed to me. I said, "What is this for?" and uLadi replied, "On this paper we have written some words." I said, "What words?" and he replied, "The words we have been talking. Now we want you to draw a line on this paper and that will mean that we agree to do what you said." So I made a mark on that paper. The whitemen were happy and went away. I believe uLadi left the country that very day but uTomusoni and Maguire remained behind.

'Some moons later, however, one of the whitemen, Reni Tela [Rennie-Taylor] who was at the kraal came to see me with a newspaper which he said was telling everybody that I had given my country away to Lodzi and had done this by signing an agreement with Ladi. I did not believe him at first, but when I called the uMfundisi Helm to tell me what the paper said and he confirmed the words of Reni Tela, I was greatly worried.

'I made enquiries about the activities of these men. I found that Maguire had followed uLadi but Tomusoni was still in the country. I called Tomusoni and asked him about what the paper said. Tomusoni denied to me that the paper claimed that I had sold my country to them. I told Tomusoni that I wanted that paper brought back to me so that I could see it.

'It was at this time that I discovered something that hurt my heart very much indeed. I discovered that Lotshe, the senior induna in the land, the man who was to me what uMncumbata was to my father, had betrayed me and the Amandebele people. I discovered that Lotshe had been bribed by Tomusoni and had agreed to give me advice so that I would do what Tomusoni and his friends wanted. It was only then that I understood why Lotshe had been such a good friend of these whitemen. I realized why Lotshe had advised me to deal only with these whitemen; why he had pleaded for the life of that magician uMaguire; why he had pleaded that I should give Shippard the road. I also found out that it was Lotshe who had advised the whitemen to offer guns to me instead of gold coins which he knew I did not care for because I had no use for them.

'Although it hurt my heart to do it, because Lotshe had fought bravely for the nation in the past, I decided that he and all his wives and children, nieces and nephews should be wiped out. I ordered the Mbesu regiment to wipe him out completely so that everybody would know what we do to traitors who abuse their positions and use them to gain personal wealth. Lotshe had received three hundred pieces of gold from Tomusoni. More than three hundred members of his family were killed for this. All his kraals were burnt and I confiscated all his cattle.

'When Tomusoni heard about this he fled from the country like a wild deer, leaving all his belongings behind.

'I then caused to be published in a newspaper which they told me was called *The Bechuanaland News and Malmani Chronicle*, a notice which said,

I hear it is published in the newspapers that I have granted a concession in all my country to Charles Dunnell Rudd, Rochfort Maguire, and Francis Robert Thompson. As there is a great misunderstanding about this, all action in respect of the said concession is hereby suspended, pending an investigation to be made by me in my country.

Signed

Lobengula

Royal Kraal
Matebeleland
18 January 1889

'I said that I wanted those words to be written in all the newspapers that whitemen read. Some whitemen later came to me with newspapers, in which they said my words had been written.

'It was at this time that I decided to send the indunas Babiyane and uMtshede to go beyond the seas to the land of the whitemen and see the white Queen for themselves. I wanted them to be my mouth, eyes and ears and ascertain that there was such a person as the white Queen. I gave them a letter to carry to the Queen and told them to give it to her if she was there.

'Since uJoni had once informed me that the Queen was feared by the Amaputukezi, I asked her, in my letter, to tell the Amaputukezi not to interfere with my country. But I also told Mtshede and Babiyane words to tell the white Queen which I did not put in the letter. I told them to tell her that I was much troubled by her people coming to ask for permission to dig gold in my country and I wanted her to tell me what to do with them because they were worrying me.

'I asked a whiteman uMondi [Maund] to accompany Mtshede and Babiyane to this far-off country, since he knew the road and it was his home. I chose Babiyane to go on this journey because he has a good tongue and speaks very well, but Mtshede I selected for his good memory because he remembers many things long after most people have forgotten them. Both these men are here and I would like them to tell you what happened on their journey.'

It was Babiyane who spoke. He spoke sitting down, because no man should stand in front of the king, for he would thereby stand higher than his king which would be a breach of etiquette.

'*Bayete! Bayete! Bayete!* You are like the Heavens!' roared the council as a prelude to Babiyane's speech.

Then he said, 'The Bull Elephant our Father, Eater of Men, the Great and Noble Lion uLobengula and my fathers. What the Lion has told you is true. Mtshede and I were selected to go on a mission to the white Queen's home across the seas as the mouth, eyes and ears of the king. The king gave us money—six hundred pieces of gold to pay for our journey and he told uMondi to be our guide on this journey. After receiving medicines to fortify us and after calling on the spirits of our ancestors to guard and protect us on this long journey, since we were to be the first sons of the Amandebele to cross the seas, we took leave of our great king and left our land.

'We travelled to Cape Town by the longer road that goes through the Transvaal instead of taking the shorter road to Khama's country because uMondi feared that, in Khama's country, we might be stopped and prevented from going on our journey by Lodzi's men. When we arrived in Kimberley Mondi told us that he had seen Lodzi who had tried to persuade him not to take us to England. We travelled on and arrived in Cape Town. We were amazed not only by the whiteman's village but also by the sea. It was so big! Everywhere we looked we saw nothing but water, water and more water. But before we left our country, the king had called us and told us that if a man goes to other people's countries and finds things that are not in his country he does not keep on saying au! au! au! in amazement because this shows clearly to everybody that such things are not in his country. The king asked us to remember this in our travels. Now, in Cape Town, we saw the sea and it was truly a wonderful sight. But remembering the words of the king, Mtshede only said, "Ah! Today the river is in flood."

'Here Mondi also told us that the big induna uGavuna Robinson was refusing to give us the road to cross the sea and go to England and wanted to see us the following day. When we saw him, he wanted us to tell him what we were going to do or say in England. We told him that we had a message from our king to deliver to the white Queen. He then said that we should tell him that message. We replied that we could not tell anyone this message as we had been instructed by our king to deliver the message only to the Queen. The induna said that he was the Queen's induna and it was their custom that all messages to the Queen were given to him. We replied and said that our custom prevented us from telling anyone except the person concerned, a message from our king. The induna stuck to his custom and we stuck to ours. He said that he would not give us the road to England. We left him.

'The following day he called us again and repeated that unless we told him our message he would not give us the road. We told him again that we could not tell any man the words of our king. He said that we should now return home and tell our king that we had been unable to get to England. We told him that we would not do that as we must carry out the instructions of our king. He then told us that it was very cold in England and we would not like the weather there. We said that being cold was a small thing compared to disobeying the instructions of our king.

'The induna then said that if we were afraid of returning to our country we could live in the Cape and he would protect us. We thanked him for his concern for us and told him that we had one desire, and that was to carry out our instructions by proceeding to England to deliver our message to the Queen.

'On the third day, however, Mondi, who appears to have received some news from his country which made him less hostile to Lodzi suggested that we should show the letter we carried to the Queen's induna since the whitemen who had written it for our king knew what it said anyway. We agreed to do this in order to have the road. We decided, however, that we would not tell the Queen's induna about the verbal message to the Queen.

76

'When the induna saw our letter he was very pleased and asked us if this was all we were going to say in England. We told him that the king had also sent us to see if there really was a person called the white Queen. He laughed.

'We were given the road and were joined by Selous on our voyage to England. Although we knew that this Selous was there to watch us, he spoke our language well so we did not mind having him with us.

'We arrived in London and saw many wonderful things, but we remembered the words of the Lion and did not look amazed by what we saw even though everything was really amazing to us. We were very well received by the English, who are very nice people in their own country.

'We saw the Queen's biggest induna and he took us to the Queen. When she entered the room where we were waiting, I was nervous and stricken with fear and I crouched on the floor with my hands on the stomach and the Queen laughed and said: "Rise, O Babiyane!" And I stood up and saw, hau! She was very small, very, very small, no higher than that calabash of beer but terrible to look at—a great ruler. We gave her the king's letter and also told her the king's message that her people were worrying him by asking for permission to dig gold in his country.

'We were told to return a few days later for a reply. In the meantime we were taken to see the big guns and the soldiers of the Queen. They tried to fire these guns but some of them jammed and would not make any sound.

'We were also taken to see the great big bank where the Queen keeps all her gold. We saw a lot of gold and Mtshede asked why the Queen took the trouble to send her people all the way to our country to look for more gold when she already had so much.

'After that we returned to the Queen's house where we were given a letter and messages to carry back to our king.

The white Queen told us that in her letter to our king, she had written these words, "The Queen has heard the words of Lobengula and she was glad to receive these messengers who had told her that Lobengula was much troubled by whitemen who come into his country to ask to dig gold and that he begs for advice and help. Lobengula is the ruler of his country and the Queen does not interfere with the Government of that country but as Lobengula desires advice, the Queen wishes Lobengula to understand that Englishmen who have gone to Matebeleland to ask leave to dig for stones have not gone with the Queen's authority. The Queen advises Lobengula not to grant hastily concessions of land or leave to dig. A King gives a stranger an ox but not a whole herd of cattle, otherwise he will have nothing left when others come."

'The white Queen also gave us a verbal message to our king. She said, "Tell the King uLobengula that he should not let anyone dig for gold in his country except to dig for him as his servant." We thanked the Queen for her words.

'Members of the Aborigines' Protection Society also gave us a letter advising the king against signing away his property.

'Before we left England, we told the Queen's biggest induna that since we had been sent on a friendly visit by our king, it was expected that we should take back to our king women to be his wives, from the land we had visited, and so cement in a very real way the bonds of friendship we had created between our two countries. There was no response from the Amangisi.

'We returned to our country and reported these things to the Lion, our king.'

Lobengula then continued, 'After the return of my indunas from England, I caused a letter to be sent to the Queen in which I spoke these words:

The white people are troubling me much about gold. If the Queen hears that I have given away the whole country, it is not so. I have no one in my country who knows how to write; I do not understand what all this is about. I thank the Queen for the word which my messengers gave me by mouth, that the Queen says I am not to let anyone dig for gold in my country except to dig for me as my servants.

'I also told the Queen that since she had once said that I could have her representative living with me here whenever I was ready to receive him, I now wanted such a person to come and was ready to receive him.

'The white Queen replied to my letter saying:

The Queen has kept in mind the letter sent by Lobengula and has now desired that Mr Moffat [that is uJoni] whom she trusts should be the one to tell Lobengula what she has done for him and what she advises him to do.

Wherever gold is, or wherever it is reported to be, it is impossible for Lobengula to exclude white men and therefore the wisest and safest course for him is to agree, not with one or two white men separately but with one approved body. If he does not agree with one set of people, there will be endless disputes among the white men and he will have all his time taken up in deciding their quarrels.

The Queen therefore approves of the concession made by Lobengula to some white men who were represented by Messrs Rudd, Maguire and Thompson. The Queen has caused enquiry to be made respecting these persons and is satisfied that they are men who will fulfil their undertakings. The Queen thinks Lobengula is acting wisely in carrying out his undertaking.

The Queen understands that Lobengula does not like deciding disputes among white men. This is very wise as these disputes take up much time and Lobengula cannot understand the laws and customs of white people. The Queen thinks it would be wise to entrust to that body of white men of whom Mr Jameson is now the principal representative in Matebeleland the duty of deciding disputes and keeping the peace among white people in his country.

The Queen understands that Lobengula wishes to have someone from her residing with him. The Queen has therefore directed her trusted servant Mr Moffat to stay with the chief as long as he wishes.

'Now, after receiving this message, my father and gallant indunas of the great Amandebele Nation, does it surprise anyone that I never thought it worth the time to write to this Queen again? I had done everything humanly possible to show these people that I did not recognize what they called the Rudd Concession. I had made a public notice suspending it; I had asked Tomusoni to bring it back to me so that I could examine it; I had ordered the induna who had championed it to be executed. I had told the Queen that her people were worrying me by asking permission to dig gold in my country and she had replied with a true word that I should not give everything to one man for a king gives a stranger one ox but never the whole herd, and said further that I should not let anyone dig unless he was digging for me as my servant. Now when I assure this Queen that I never gave anyone the right to dig minerals in my land she replies saying I did right to give this privilege to Ladi, Tomusoni and Maguire and I should let Jemisoni decide disputes among whitemen in my country. What kind of foolishness was this?'

There were cries of 'It was madness!' 'Yes, real madness!' 'White people are all mad!' from the indunas.

Lobengula continued, 'The Queen had also once informed me that I should tell her when I wanted her to send a personal representative to live with me in my country. I told her that I now wanted such a person to come. Does she send this person? No. She tells me that Joni is her representative. When she told me she would send a representative here, was Joni not in this country? How then, had he become her representative all of a sudden? We of course did not mean Joni. We wanted somebody from herself. We counted Joni on our side; after all he enjoyed the privileges of a prince among us. We wanted someone who was a man of honour who would not tell us lies or lie about us.'

Here Mzilikazi interrupted his son and said, 'My son, you never really understood these whitemen. Do you know that the last letter you received from the Queen, the one that said you had done well to give the rights to Ladi, Tomusoni and Maguire was not the Queen's letter?'

'Au! How could that be?'

'Yes, when the messenger bearing the letter from the Queen arrived in our land, Jemisoni opened the letter, read it, tore it up and wrote one himself and then signed the name of his Queen. uJoni knew all this when he read Jemisoni's letter to you saying that it had come from the Queen.'

Cries of 'Shocking!' 'Dishonourable', and 'Cheats' from the indunas followed this revelation. And when these cries had died down Lobengula continued.

'How could one deal with such men? What kind of men were they? Men who did not hesitate to forge even their Queen's signature!'

A voice said, 'They were civilized. That is what civilized men do!'

Lobengula continued, 'The truth is that whatever I did or

81

said in the matter was immaterial and unimportant. These men were after my country. I was like a fly. Have you ever watched a chameleon catch a fly? It comes slowly and noiselessly, one hesitating step at a time until it is very close, then it flickers its tongue out and the fly is gone. These men were like the chameleon taking one step at a time towards me and my country. One dart of the tongue and my country and I would be gone.'

Mzilikazi continued, 'Why did you not fight?'

'Did my father say fight? I knew very well that Mandebele spears were no match for the whiteman's guns.'

'But in the end you had to fight, didn't you?'

'Yes, in the end I was forced to fight. But my policy was to avoid fighting if that was possible. I knew that the whitemen wanted me to order the slaughter of a few of their number so that they would send an impi against me. I knew what that meant—another war like the one we fought with the Boers in the Transvaal. Our men would have fought gallantly and bravely but only to meet certain death from the fire-spitting guns of a small impi of whitemen. As sure as the sun rises in the east and sets in the west we would have been forced to burn our kraals and trek away in flight as we did in the Transvaal. Then the whitemen would have remained, taking over the whole country as the Boers did across the Transvaal. Our only chance lay in avoiding war. I knew that most of the whitemen around my kraal were crooks, but I thought I could trust the word of their indunas and their Queen. So I dealt with their indunas and their Queen and hoped that as people of honour we might arrive at an acceptable solution which would avoid war and preserve the country with honour for the Amandebele.

'I did not mind letting them dig their hole, provided they were not too many. I was interested in the guns Ladi offered in payment. But why did they tell lies that I had sold them my country and why did their Queen not believe me when I told her I had not given anyone the right to dig gold in my country? Now we learn that the Queen never wrote that letter and that Jemisoni forged her signature and said all those things. What could anyone have done with such dishonourable men? Just look at Joni. He and his father preached to us about God until our ears were full. They said that their God wanted people to be honest, kind and good and not kill many people as the Amandebele did. Was it being honest first, to trick me into signing a paper for his Queen and now to read a letter to me saying it was written by his Queen when he knew very well that the letter had been written by Jemisoni?'

Mzilikazi now made another disclosure, 'My son, you have not yet heard the worst about these Christians. That uMfundisi uHelemu: you trusted him. You listened to his advice when he told you to deal with one group of whitemen, the group of Lodzi. You believed this to be the honest advice of a man who had no axe to grind in the matter.'

'Yes, my father, that is so indeed.'

'Well, uHelemu was in the employ of Lodzi. He was in Lodzi's group.'

The indunas greeted this news with loud and indignant cries of 'Au! Au! Even missionaries! Au! Was all this talk about Christianity to make us soft so that they could steal our land?'

'Yes, that is why they made you close your eyes when they prayed—so that when you opened your eyes—the land would be gone!'

CHAPTER SEVEN

Chaminuka's Death

Cecil Rhodes once more took the stand at the altar rails of the church in Bishop's Stortford. 'I was, naturally, extremely gratified by the success of my mission to Lobengula. Rudd, Thompson and Maguire had done a magnificent job. Sir Hercules Robinson, the Governor, was also very pleased with our success. Although he grumbled a little over our promise to supply rifles and ammunition to Lobengula because this was contrary to the General Act of the Brussels Conference to which Britain was a signatory, I soon put his mind at rest by assuring him that we would keep that part of the bargain a very close secret and that no great harm would arise from the possession of rifles by the Matebele, since natives always fired a rifle with their eyes closed.

'With Lobengula's concession in my pocket, I set about forming a company to take over the country and to apply for a Royal Charter granting us permission not only to exploit minerals but also to play a part in the politics and administration of the country on the pattern of the East India Company, the East Africa Company and the Royal Niger Company.

'In order to do this effectively, it was necessary for me to strengthen our claim in Matebeleland and silence a few of our loud-mouthed and more persistent rivals who had an assortment of concessions—real and imaginary—by inviting

84

some of them to join us and buying, outright, the claims of others. One of the claims I bought in this way was that of Frederick Courteney Selous, the famous hunter. I mention his concession here because I have been charged, in this church, with dispossessing Lobengula of his land and usurping his country. This charge, no doubt, assumes that Lobengula was complete master and undisputed ruler of all the land lying between the Limpopo and the Zambezi rivers and bounded by the Portuguese coastal strip in the east and Bechuanaland in the west. I know that this is the popular and more widely held idea of the extent of Lobengula's country because I helped, for my own ends, to create it.

'After the signing of the Rudd Concession, it suited me; indeed it was in my very best interests to claim that Lobengula held sway over as large a part of Africa as I could make anyone believe. I was certain that just as the Moffat treaty would keep foreign powers out of this territory, the Rudd Concession would keep out all my British rivals. So, I spread the idea that Lobengula was lord and master over the whole country when I knew perfectly well that there were tribes in Mashonaland and Manicaland who did not acknowledge him as their king.

'Selous, who spoke several native languages and whose countless hunting safaris brought him into contact with many native chiefs and tribes, enabling him to know more about the geography of this part of Africa than any white man alive, had a mineral concession from a Makorekore chief, which I bought because I did not want him to put his claim in public and expose the fact that Lobengula did not rule over as large a country as I claimed he did. Such a view, expressed by a man of Selous' reputation and ability would have considerably undermined my Rudd Concession. So I gave him £2,000 to seal his mouth. Therefore, when you accuse me of dispossessing Lobengula of his land, please remember that it was only a very small part of what is known today as Rhodesia, that Lobengula actually ruled over. Selous is here; no doubt, you would like him to confirm what I have said and to tell you some of the things he saw in Matebeleland.'

Selous stood up and walked to the altar. He still had that sprightly gait, alert eyes and athletic physique which had made him the most famous hunter south of the Equator and the best shot in all Africa.

'What Rhodes says is true,' he began, showing the discomfort of a man more at home on a horse than on a public platform, 'although Lobengula claimed that his land stretched as far as his impis had marched, this did not cover all the country that we attributed to him. There were areas in that country where the Matebele were not known, had never been, and their claim of sovereignty would have been strongly challenged and contested.

'There was the Makorekore chief Mapondera in the Mount Darwin area from whom I got a mineral concession. He did not know who Lobengula was and had never even heard of the Matebele. There were other chiefs in Manicaland like Mutasa and Makoni who had never fought with or been conquered by Lobengula. There was his kinsman, Ngungunyana, the descendant of Sotshangane who, like Mzilikazi, had broken away from the Zulu nation in the south. He never accepted or recognized Lobengula's suzerainty over him. Even some Mazezuru tribes in central Mashonaland were never subjects of the Matebele, although they knew of their existence and called them "Madzviti".

'This is not to say, however, that the Matebele had no power over some tribes in Mashonaland. They had. They conquered a number of tribes and terrorized some parts of the country. The cry, "Hayo Madzviti!"—"There are the Matebele!"—was a widely spread cry of terror and doom

86

which sent most Mashona tribesmen running helter-skelter for shelter to their burrows and caves in the mountains.

'The Matebele did not always attack other tribes for sport, as is often said. They did it, at times, out of sheer necessity. Fighting and war was, of course, in their blood. They existed and were organized as a people for nothing else. But it also happens that they had chosen to settle on land that agriculturally was most unsuitable and—singularly unproductive. The rainfall was very low and droughts were very frequent. Cattle grazing, the only thing for which this part of the country was generally suited, was limited by scarcity of water and proximity to the tsetse-fly belt.

'Since beef was their staple diet and a low rainfall conspired with a poor sandy soil to make the growing of grain in large quantities wellnigh, if not, impossible, the Matebele attacked and sacked other tribes more to replenish their supply of cattle and grain than for the sheer fun of spilling blood. It was because of a famine caused by drought and a lung disease which decimated hundreds of cattle that three military expeditions were sent out by Mzilikazi in 1867. One was despatched to Mashonaland and the others to Bechuanaland and the area of Lake Ngami. The first two were successful, particularly the Mashonaland Campaigns which resulted in the capture of an important Muzezuru Chief Hwata and a valuable haul of grain and cattle. So large was the booty that it took several hours for the cattle and grain-carrying captives to pass before our eyes. Poor Chief Hwata was hauled before Mzilikazi by the jubilant warriors who expected him to be executed on the spot, but Mzilikazi surprised everyone by allowing Chief Hwata to return to Mashonaland merely on condition that in future he would pay regular tribute to him.

'In time of crises—a severe drought or when rumours of an impending invasion of the country were circulating freely

—the Matabele often consulted Mashona witch-doctors and diviners. This was done in July 1866, in the time of Mzilikazi, when, as a result of a long illness, the king lost his mind somewhat, and saw hordes of Zulus under the fearful leadership of the dreaded black Napoleon Tshaka pursuing him and his people. Summoning his indunas Mzilikazi commanded them to mobilize the country and quarter all the regiments at the royal kraal. He scolded them for the unpreparedness of the Matebele to meet the invaders and the weakness of their defences.

'Thousands of Matebele warriors answered the king's call, and in battle dress marched to the royal kraal where they sang and danced while awaiting further orders. Hundreds of cattle were slaughtered to provide them with food and all along the paths were long lines of women carrying calabashes of beer for the prancing warriors. The villages were empty. Matebeleland was mobilized.

'Later, the king announced his decision to abandon Matebeleland and flee to Lake Ngami before the arrival of the invaders. He ordered his wives to pack their belongings in preparation for the trek and commanded his indunas to organize the migration to the new Matebeleland.

'A missionary doctor remonstrated with the king, begging him to dispel the hallucinations from his mind before they caused him to impose great suffering and hardship on his people. The king relented, agreeing that the trek to Lake Ngami would be hazardous for his people, and suggested crossing the Zambezi as a more suitable destination.

'The indunas then timidly and fearfully at first, but more confidently later, recounted with gusto and great eloquence, punctuated by thundering praises of their king, the story of their flight from Zululand under the unmatched leadership of Mzilikazi. Carried by the exuberance of his own eloquence and sincerity an old induna wept as he implored the king not to flee but to stand firm and fight. The king was deeply moved.

'At this moment two indunas who had been sent to consult a Mashona witch-doctor captured in one of the Matebele raids, stepped forward and reported that the diviner had cast his bones and by the positions the bones took when they fell, had seen that enemies of the Matebele would enter the country from the south. He therefore advised the Matebele to watch their southern border carefully. The Mashona diviner had further told them that there was no danger whatsoever from a Zulu army.

'Mzilikazi cancelled the migration to the west. The indunas, warriors and all leaped to the sky, danced, shouted and sang his praises.

'Years later, as I led the Pioneer Column into Mashonaland from the south, I could not help remembering the Mashona witch-doctor's "watch your southern border" advice to the Matebele.

'The Matebele were not always as successful in capturing Mashona chiefs as they were with Hwata. One that eluded them many times was Chaminuka. Chaminuka was a chief who lived at a place called Chitungwiza, a few miles from Salisbury on the old Charter Road, between the Mufuri and Manyame rivers.

'Chaminuka was not only a powerful chief; he was also a seer credited with possession of supernatural powers. At his court, in Chitungwiza, he sat on an ox-hide that was nailed into a flat rock by wooden pegs. He was so famous for his ability to cause rain to fall that many chiefs, throughout the land, felt obliged to pay homage to him at the beginning of each rainy season.

'Lobengula heard of him and sent his soldiers to capture him and bring him to Bulawayo, but each time the Matebele warriors approached Chaminuka's village, a cloud of mist and fog would appear before them and they would not know whence they came or where they were going. This happened many times until Lobengula decided to befriend himself to the great seer of Chitungwiza and instead of sending impis to attack him he regularly sent Chaminuka gifts of wives, ivory and cattle. This went on for a number of years and Chaminuka became extremely wealthy, amassing a great quantity of ivory, cattle and grain as each day gifts were showered upon him by all and sundry. His people, free from Matebele attacks, also became very prosperous.

'Among the women Lobengula sent to be Chaminuka's wives was a girl named Baveya. Baveya was born in Matebeleland from among the Amahole captured after a raid. Lobengula's sister took a liking for her and sent her, as a little child, to the home of the Rev. and Mrs C. D. Helm, where she was brought up and learnt to speak English fluently. In 1880, however, very much against her will, the king ordered her to be sent to Chitungwiza and to become one of the great seer's wives.

'In 1883 Lobengula sent more presents and gifts to Chaminuka and also invited the seer of Chitungwiza to visit him at his capital city in Bulawayo. Although Chaminuka was aware that he would not return to his home alive, because he had been warned that he would die in a far-off place, among strange people, his curiosity overcame him and he accepted Lobengula's invitation.

'The old man set out on his journey with a retinue of about fifteen people, among whom were his wife Baveya and a son aged about fifteen years old. Chaminuka never reached Bulawayo.

'After sending his messengers to invite Chaminuka to visit him in Bulawayo, Lobengula called an impi and told them, "You go and meet the wizard at Shangani River. Kill him and all who are with him. Let no one escape. Then hasten on and go to Chitungwiza and kill all his people, destroy their villages and bring his cattle and ivory here."

'So when Chaminuka and his party arrived at the Shangani River, the Matebele impi was already there. The impi kept out of sight and only a few indunas came forward as if to greet the great seer and welcome him into their country.

'Several years later, I heard the sad story of what happened at the river from Baveya's own lips. She told me that when the Matebele indunas appeared, she quickly sensed danger and said, "They are going to kill you; I know the Matebele. I grew up among them. They are going to kill you. Run! Please run. I can see blood in their eyes; run! Chaminuka, run!" But the old man replied, "As old as I am, how far would I get even if I ran? Baveya, my wife, if my day has come, Chaminuka does not fear to die. But tell my son who is young and whose feet are still light to creep away among the bushes before they are here and carry the news to my people at home."

'Chaminuka's son disappeared among the bushes and ran back home as fast as his legs could carry him. On the way, however, so Baveya told me, he saw a lion. But as this lion prepared to pounce upon him and tear him to pieces another lion appeared as if from nowhere and attacked it. The boy ran even faster, leaving the two lions grappling with each other, behind. The old people later declared that the second lion was a *mhondoro yemudzimu*—a guardian ancestral spirit lion—whose function is to protect descendants. The boy ran until he arrived at Chitungwiza with his sad news. The people, thus warned, immediately fled across the Mhanyame River into the hills between the Mazoe and Nyaguwe rivers, but they left most of their grain and some cattle behind.

'At Shangani River Chaminuka's party was soon surrounded by Lobengula's impi. Twelve Matebele warriors pounced upon Chaminuka and threw their spears into his body, but Baveya said that the spears would neither penetrate his body nor scratch it. Instead, their blades broke and fell to the ground and the warriors' arms began to swell like inflated tubes. The Matebele were amazed and terrified, but the king's order must be obeyed and so twelve more Matebele warriors again obeyed their king's command to kill the wizard of Chitungwiza; but this time they all dropped down dead before they could touch him. When she told me this story, Baveya continued:

Then Chaminuka opened his mouth and said, "If you give me your word that you will not touch these people in my company, I will tell you how you can kill me." The Matebele indunas swore, by their Mlimu, that they would spare the lives of all who were with him. Then the seer of Chitungwiza said, "You let my musicians play soft *marimba* music on *mbira* instruments. Then select a youth who has not yet touched a woman to spear me, facing the north. I shall die. But before I die and join my ancestors let me tell you this: because you have dared to lay hands on me your land shall be dry; you shall suffer for lack of rain and many of your children and cattle will die of drought. There will be frequent droughts in your land. Furthermore, you shall not rule over this land much longer because there will come people who have no knees and have red ears. On this very spot where you kill me they will conquer you. They will rule over you.

'When I am dead, let my musicians continue to play the *mbira* night and day until I have been buried a full moon. To lift my body, after my death, use the stalks of a mealie plant. That is all. I Chaminuka now wish to depart and join the spirits of my ancestors."

They did as he had said. A little boy who had not yet

92

touched a woman advanced with a spear; facing north to Chitungwiza in Mashonaland and further north to "Guruuswa" from where, the Mashona believe, all men originally came. The little boy thrust his spear and the great seer of Chitungwiza died.

'To this day, Matebeleland does not have much rain and indeed the whitemen came and took over Lobengula's country, defeating him at Shangani in the war of 1893, as Chaminuka had prophesied.

'After killing Chaminuka, Lobengula's impi rushed to Chitungwiza and found the villages deserted. They saw only a few strangers who had arrived at the kraal to pay homage to Chaminuka. These people were all killed by the Matebele. The impi then went to chief Musikaguva and camped near his kraal. This chief was a vassal of Lobengula and, in fact, kept some of Lobengula's cattle. His people brought beer and food to the Matebele soldiers, who appeared to be on very friendly terms with them. Musikaguva's people went to sleep not suspecting anything.

'At dawn, however, they woke up to find all their villages surrounded by Matebele warriors. The impi fell upon them and slaughtered them all—men, women, and children. Children were seized by the ankles and their brains dashed out against stones. The only reason given for this massacre was that Lobengula had ordered it.

'Four months after the death of Chaminuka I passed through the deserted villages of Chitungwiza. Some of the villages had been burnt but others were still standing, and although all the granaries had been overturned many of them were still stacked with mealies and corn. I saw some remains of the dead. In the fields the rice and corn had been harvested before the flight but the groundnuts and sweet potatoes were still in the ground.

'Baveya's life among the Mashona people must have been to her liking because she ran away from Matebeleland and returned to live among the Mashona. In 1887, I saw her in the Lomagundi area of north-western Mashonaland. It was then that she related to me the story of her great husband's death.

'I have wandered a little from my main purpose for speaking to you which was to tell you that Lobengula was not the undisputed master of the whole country we now call Rhodesia. I think I have told you enough to show you that there were other people who had greater physical as well as spiritual power over tribes in parts of what we called Lobengula's land.'

Selous took his seat and once more Rhodes continued his story. 'After eliminating the competition of rivals in Matebeleland, I turned to the task of securing a charter. In London, I encountered opponents of a different sort who, because of character and integrity, could not be "fixed" or "squared" in the usual way. These were that implacable opponent of European enterprise in Africa and self-appointed champion of the African, the Rev. John Mackenzie, the Aborigines' Protection Society and, for reasons I have never been able to discover, the London Chamber of Commerce. They were all opposed to the grant of a charter, which, they alleged, would only enable me to oppress and exploit the natives. They enlisted support of some of the most eminent and influential members of both houses of Parliament, like the Duke of Fife, Earl Grey, Sir T. Fowell-Buxton, Joseph Chamberlain and the able Labouchere, and persuaded them to form a committee to resist any grant of a charter to me.

'But I had friends, too. On my side were Lord Rothschild, the father-in-law of Lord Rosebery, who later became Prime Minister, and Sir Hercules Robinson who took it upon himself to convert the leading officials of the Colonial Office to my side. I was advised to include among the directors of the proposed Chartered Company men of social and political standing, and so invited, among others, the Duke of Abercorn, the Duke of Fife, a son-in-law of the Prince of Wales, and Albert Grey, a grandson of a former Prime Minister. These men agreed to serve on my board and things appeared to be going my way when the news that Lobengula had repudiated the Rudd Concession, executed his induna Lotshe and threatened to kill Thompson who had, as a result, run away from the country, reached me. Since Thompson is here I will let him tell you what happened.'

'After the signing of the Rudd Concession,' Thompson began, 'Lobengula appeared to favour and trust us more than he did the other white men at his court. He consulted Maguire and me about everything, and at our suggestion sent us with an impi to prevent a party of rivals which included Alfred Haggard, brother of Rider Haggard, the famous novelist, from crossing the border into his country. But so many people kept on telling Lobengula that he had, in fact, sold his country through our deal with him, that, I think, he began to believe it. I did my best to deny this and offered to publish a statement emphasizing that the king had only granted us a mineral concession and nothing more. I believe Lobengula would have accepted my offer and let the matter rest where it was if it had not been for Maund who had worked his way to Lobengula's favour and was whispering all sorts of stories to him. A Boer delegation which called on him and told him, point blank, that he had sold his country to us, appears to have succeeded in stirring him to action.

'By a notice in the Bechuanaland newspaper, he suspended our concession and executed, with all his relations, Lotshe, the induna who had been our best friend and champion. Maguire and I soon found ourselves regarded almost as hostages to be put to death if something went wrong or if our party were unable to obey the king's order to return the concession for his inspection. Bored with his unchanging diet of beef and beer, bored with the company he kept, bored with just doing nothing except smell the stink and stench of the royal kraal, Maguire slipped away from Matebeleland, leaving me to hold the fort alone.

'I would have gladly left with him but for the fact that I had promised Rhodes to remain in Matebeleland until the charter was granted, and he had signified this by sending me a telegram with the code word "Runnymede". A few days after Maguire's departure Rhodes' message—"Runnymede" —arrived, and I felt free to leave the country. But what actually made me leave was the hint I received, possibly from the king himself, that my life was in danger.

'One morning I was driving to Hope Fountain—that is what the missionaries called their station near the royal kraal—to consult with Helm on a number of things. I had not driven more than a few hundred yards when a native, on a grey horse, rode up behind me and shouted, "Tomusoni! Tomusoni! The king says the killing is not yet over." I knew, of course, that by "the killing" he was referring to the massacre of Lotshe and over three hundred of his relatives, and believed that the king was giving me an opportunity to save my life.

'There and then, there appeared in front of me a number of Matebele warriors in battle dress, who apparently had been hiding in the bush close by. Cutting loose my fastest horse from the team, I jumped on its back and without even a saddle rode south. I had no hat, let alone food or water, but I rode so fast that by sundown I was in the Kalahari desert. I spent the night in a tree for fear of lions and rode on the next day. But my horse was tired and foundered. I left it where it fell and, walking or running, covered forty miles before I found a water hole.

'The next day I fortunately came on a trader with a small mule wagon, who gave me a lift to Shoshong from where I made my way to Mafeking.'

When Thompson finished telling his story, Rhodes took up his tale again. 'I, of course, took steps to see that Lobengula's repudiation of the Rudd Concession was not known in London. My efforts to get a charter were crowned with success when this was granted on the 29th October 1888. It authorized us to make treaties, promulgate laws, preserve the peace, maintain a police force and acquire new concessions. We were empowered to make roads, railways, harbours, or undertake other public works, own or charter ships, engage in mining or other industry, establish banks, make land grants, and carry on any lawful commerce, trade, pursuit or business. We were authorized to do all this on territory that was defined, simply, as north of the Cape Colony and the Transvaal and west of Portuguese East Africa.'

Rev. Rhodes then said, 'How could a charter from the British Crown empower you to maintain a police force and levy taxes, establish banks, industries, etc., in Lobengula's country? Was it assumed that the Queen had authority in all Africa?'

'No. It was not assumed that the Queen had authority all over Africa, but it was assumed that among the various groups brought together by my Chartered Company, which I called the British South Africa Company, there were men who already held concessions from Lobengula which gave them authority to exercise these powers and that they would acquire new concessions that would empower them to exercise others. The charter gave permission to these British subjects, and these only, to exercise any rights that Lobengula might concede.'

'What you are saying is that the Queen assumed that you

97

and your friends had been given certain rights by Lobengula and the charter merely permitted you to exercise those rights.'

'Yes, that is correct.'

'But you knew and those who spoke for the Queen also knew that, at the most, you had merely been granted permission to dig for gold, not to do all the other things that the charter authorized you to do.'

'Yes, the charter recognized this. That is why it permitted us to enter into further negotiations with Lobengula to secure his permission to do the other things. But it also gave us in advance, permission to do those things if and when we obtained Lobengula's consent.'

'And yet you went ahead and did the things the charter authorized you without securing Lobengula's further permission.'

'Yes, we did.'

'Why did you have to get a charter to exercise a right you had been granted by a sovereign king—Lobengula? Was his permission, if it was ever given, not enough?'

'It was enough, but a British Royal Charter protected us from foreign competitors.'

'So you secured a concession you knew to be of doubtful validity from Lobengula and decided to exceed its terms. You then got the British Crown to clothe your actions in a myth of legality and respectability, authorizing you to exceed your powers by the ruse of pretending that they were merely permitting you in advance to exercise any rights you might subsequently negotiate with Lobengula. You, on your part, then went ahead and acted as if the British Government had actually given you the right to do all those things they said you could do after you had received Lobengula's permission; and they, for their part, turned a blind eye to everything illegal that you did not bothering to ascertain whether you had, in fact, got further permission from Lobengula.'

'Yes, that is so.'

'I do not know who was more crooked—you or the British Government.'

CHAPTER EIGHT

The Talk about a Road

THE WHITE MAN'S VERSION

Rhodes was the narrator again in the church in Bishop's Stortford. 'I found myself working on our plans for the occupation of Mashonaland, even before the Royal Charter creating the British South Africa Company had been signed, sealed and delivered. I knew that there was no time to lose. Our position in Matebeleland filled me with anxiety. Thompson's flight had left us without a representative at Lobengula's court. There were several concession hunters still bent on making trouble for us. There was also the distinct possibility and likelihood that Lobengula would refuse to accept the rifles and money that were due to him in terms of our concession. The reaction of public opinion in England to such a move by Lobengula would have been disastrous to us. I was also not unaware of the designs that the Portuguese still had on the country. I therefore came to the conclusion that to assure our position it was necessary to obtain effective possession of Mashonaland in the coming winter. This could not be achieved by merely sending one or two prospecting parties. I felt it was necessary to send, without delay, as large a nucleus of white settlers as possible.

'I believed, however, that a great deal would depend on whether or not Lobengula accepted the rifles due to be delivered to him. If he accepted them, he could hardly claim later that he had repudiated the agreement. The rifles were ready to be despatched, but my problem was who would take them to Lobengula? I was strongly tempted to make the trip myself, but it was quite clear that with so many things happening at the same time, I would not be able to go. I thought of sending Rudd but he was most unfortunately sick at this time. My mind then hit on Dr. Jameson's name. Yes, Dr. Jameson, he was my man! But, would he agree to go?

'I immediately went to see him and to persuade him to make the trip. He refused, saying that he had the interests of other people to consider—his patients. He could not just forget all about them while he went gallivanting in the bundu, on other people's business. I tried to show him that this was not, in fact, "other people's business" but that as a loyal Englishman, the building of a British Empire was also his business. I appealed to him as a friend to help me out, because my future plans depended on the success of this mission. I told him that he needed a holiday and that this trip was the best way of taking one. I used every argument I could think of. He did not appear to be impressed. I told him that all the bright boys who wanted to get rich quickly had their eyes on the north because that is where the future was, and a man who got in on the ground floor with an allotment of shares, could not go wrong. I spoke of the fun and excitement of a trip to Matebeleland and the romance of an encounter with a real, live, genuine savage king. This, I think, appealed to him more, and he promised to think the matter over. We agreed to discuss the proposition again the following day.

'The next day I found Jameson a different man: he had changed completely. Confronted with the choice between a regular, sedate, humdrum life of an assured and relatively uneventful medical career and an uncertain but glorious life of adventure, pulsating with excitement, danger and romance, he instinctively chose the latter. I am sure he did not care very much for personal wealth. So he agreed to leave within a few days for Matebeleland with 500 rifles and 500,000 rounds of ammunition. He was accompanied by a young doctor, Rutherford Harris, who had contracted to convey the rifles to the king's kraal. Jameson is here; I will let him tell you himself what happened.'

All eyes turned on the bald little doctor whose dash, bravado and good humour had made him one of the most loyal, intimate, likeable and colourful trouble-shooters, though some will say, trouble-makers, among Rhodes' friends.

'We began our journey to Lobengula's land,' said the doctor, 'on 3 February 1889. We drove 250 miles to catch up with our wagons, which had started a fortnight before. The wagons were fully stacked with food and other necessities, and we were well supplied with servants, horses, dogs, armoury, etc. We overtook our wagons at Mafeking, and from this point had to travel at the exasperating speed of an ox wagon. We headed for Shoshong in Khama's country, and I was a little worried by the thought that Khama might just take it into his head to make things difficult for us since the only reason he had been able to ward off Matebele attacks and preserve his throne was the fact that his men used guns while the Matebele fought with spears. Indeed, it was said that at their last encounter, Khama had personally shot and wounded Lobengula in the shoulder, and four sons of Mzilikazi had been killed by the Bechuana on that day. I thought that Khama might try to prevent the guns we were carrying from reaching Lobengula. I did not know, of course, that Rhodes and Shippard had already cleared this with Khama. We were allowed to pass through Bechuanaland without trouble.

'We went on to Tati where we were very hospitably entertained by Major Sam Edwards, a trader and very close confidant of the Matebele king. Major Edwards was popularly known as "Far Interior Sam" or just "Dear old Sam". He was one of the signposts on the road to Lobengula's kraal. He was born on his father's mission station among the Bechuanas and grew up among the natives, learning their language, customs, manners and ways of thinking better than any white man I know. In 1854 he accompanied the Rev. Moffat on his visit to Mzilikazi and thus became one of the first two white men to enter Matebeleland. Over the years Mr Edwards became an expert, a walking dictionary or encyclopaedia on all matters concerning sport or travel in Southern Africa. Both Khama and Lobengula had the most implicit trust and confidence in him, having learnt by long experience that he was an upright and honourable English gentleman on whose word they could absolutely rely, which was more than these two monarchs felt about most of the white men they met.

'We went on through the green valleys, the rugged kloofs, the towering grey granite mountains, on through the thick forests, the thorny bush, to the Manyame River and Manyame people. Here, for the first time we came into contact with the Matebele—Lobengula's border guard—tall, well-built men, proud and aristocratic. They wore magnificent ostrich-feather capes, ox-tail garters, long ox-hide shields, and carried heavy stabbing assegais. They fascinated me. I gazed at them for hours on end. Little did I know how my life would be bound up with their destiny. With the use of pink beads, brass buttons and blue calico we established friendly relations with the guard, but some forty miles on, our convoy was stopped. I decided to ride, myself, on horseback to Bulawayo and ask the king to give our wagons the road.

'On 2 April 1889, I arrived at the great oval of huts

that was called Bulawayo. It was built on a grassy plain, sparsely covered with mimosa trees and watered by a tributary of the Umguza River. Around an inner circle of the huts was the buck kraal or royal enclosure. Here the king could be found sitting on an old condensed-milk packing-case or leaning against the posts of a stage on which four slaughtered oxen were placed daily. He was about five feet eleven inches tall and must have weighed nearly nineteen stones. He walked in a most imposingly majestic manner, treading the ground slowly, deliberately and definitely, while the *imbongi* shouted his praises at each step. Sometimes he lived in his wagon, which he used to travel to other parts of his land.

'I was given an audience with the king. I have heard it said, in connection with this audience, that I was the first man, black or white, to approach Lobengula without crawling, or speaking to him, without squatting on the ground, in accordance with Matebele law or custom. This distinction must, however, go to Sir Sidney Shippard, although, as a representative of the Queen, which I was not, it would hardly have been proper for him to crawl or squat on the ground before any king. It may well be, however, that the breach in protocol was overlooked in my case because, although seated, the king's head was still higher than mine.

'I was able not only to be given the road for our wagons but also to deliver the rifles and ammunition, which were put in a trader's store on Lobengula's account. Cooper-Chadwick was appointed to look after them. Lobengula did not protest, so we concluded that he had accepted them and the concession was reinstated. Somehow the king and I understood each other. I developed a respect and liking for the old fellow, whom I thought would have been a great deal more friendly to white people if it were not for his bloodthirsty majahas. But, even then, it cannot be said that he was ever hostile to white men. My business being completed, I returned to Kimberley.

'I was back in Kimberley before Rhodes returned from London. On his return, however, he came straight to my house and, without saying anything, handed me the coded telegram—"Runnymede"—which was to tell Thompson that Rhodes' company had obtained a charter. I understood what the telegram meant. "I will go," I told him. "When can you start?" Rhodes asked. "By the post-cart tomorrow at four," I said.

'Thus, almost six months after my first trip, I found myself once more on the road to Matebeleland. Dennis Doyle and Major Maxwell, both described to me as having had experience with natives, whatever that means, were my companions. At Mafeking I found Thompson and by dint of some persuasion, got him to join our company. At Tati we picked up Lobengula's friend Sam Edwards.

'Thompson's flight had angered the king, who believed that to run away as he did, he must have been aware of some evil act he had committed. The concession was still in great danger of being completely repudiated. Lotshe, its champion, had been liquidated and discredited as "a sell out". The indunas Babiyane and Mtshede had returned with their letters from the Queen advising Lobengula not to give his whole herd to one man. Over and above all, Lobengula had been drinking excessively the liquor—brandy and champagne—provided him by concession seekers, and was suffering from a severe attack of gout and sore eyes. He was in great pain. We thus found him extremely irritable and bad-tempered when we were presented to him.

'He grumbled, "What is the use of telling me more lies? Where is uLodzi? I will not be satisfied until I see Lodzi." At the sight of Thompson he became furious, "That man is a liar and a coward," he shouted. "I do not want to talk to him."

'Our task was not only to restore friendly relations and have the concession confirmed but also, somehow, to secure permission for a party of pioneers to enter the country and commence digging. I realized that in the existing circumstances and atmosphere we would never succeed.

'So I suspended the discussion of our business and concerned myself primarily with relieving the king of his pain and restoring his health. I gave him some morphia injections and prescribed treatment for his gout. As his doctor, I was able to take liberties, to chaff him and joke with him. This impressed him and his courtiers tremendously as no other white man had treated him like that before. Fortunately he responded to my treatment. His gout and pain soon left him. He was very grateful—embarrassingly grateful to me. He made me an induna of the Matebele nation, personally dressing me in a cloak of ostrich feathers and ox-tail garters. In this attire, I accompanied him to a grand review of the impis.

'Under these changed and more favourable circumstances, I brought up the matter of our concession. He asked that I should bring it to him. I took a copy to him the following day and explained it to him clause by clause. He now took the line that he had not meant to give a general concession but to allow us to dig one hole at a time. He said that the only general part of the agreement was that no one else would be allowed to dig a hole at all. I decided, therefore, that the best policy under the circumstances, was to maintain the concession but not to insist on it and while being ready to resist any attempt to substitute it with a less sweeping agreement, to slur over its general provisions and concentrate on getting permission to dig in one hole and in so doing, legally implement it.

'It was about this time that a Captain and a Major of the Royal Horse Guards, with the Corporal-Major of the regiment and a trooper arrived at the king's kraal. They were returning the visit to London by Lobengula's indunas, Babiyane and Mtshede. When I heard that they carried a letter to Lobengula, I insisted on seeing it before it was delivered, because I did not want Lobengula to receive another letter which would be interpreted as being against us again. My fears were justified. I tore up the letter and substituted it with one of my own.

'No doubt the stature, uniforms and accoutrements of the letter-bearers attracted more attention and interest than the contents of the letter they bore. They wore red coats, breastplates, helmets and top boots. Lobengula was greatly impressed. He took off and handled one of the cuirasses, and asked them to go through the sword exercise once more. In inviting them to attend the Matebele Great Dance, he specially asked them to appear in full panoply. The Matebele crowd loved them.

'I decided to use the favourable atmosphere created by the visit of the guardsmen and my own elevation to indunaship. I told Lobengula that the hole we had dug in the south showed no payable gold and we were reluctant to look for another place around Bulawayo because we did not want to disturb Matebele villages. The king, who was in a very good mood that day, replied, "Then you had better go somewhere else." I asked if we might go east and he agreed. I took out a map on which Selous had drawn a route which avoided Matebeleland and led to the Mazoe Valley in Mashonaland. I showed it to him and asked if Selous could use some of the Matebele young men to cut the road. "Yes, he may," the king replied, but added, "go and find out where you want to make your road and then come to me; I will give you the men to make it." I thanked the king and took my leave.

'I immediately informed Rhodes that Lobengula had sanctioned our occupation of Mashonaland and soon after this, left Matebeleland with Thompson.'

Rev. Rhodes then asked, 'But had Lobengula actually done that? Had he sanctioned your occupation of Mashonaland?'

'He had said we could go and dig another hole in the east.'

'Was permission to dig a hole the same as permission to occupy a country?'

'No, it was not. But he had said that we could go there and surely while we were there it was expected that we would have some sort of an administration for the maintenance of law and order amongst our people.'

'I see. You reported your permission to dig as permission to occupy.'

Jameson took his seat and Rhodes continued his story. 'I passed on Jameson's message to the High Commissioner. Sir Henry had heard the rumour that Boers from the Transvaal were planning to enter Mashonaland and was ready to warn President Kruger that this would be regarded as an infringement of the Queen's Protectorate. He sought and received permission to authorize, when he thought fit, the entry of our pioneers into Mashonaland.

'In spite of Jameson's message, Sir Henry informed me that it would be very important, before introducing any pioneer force in Mashonaland, to ascertain clearly that its presence there would be acceptable to Lobengula and reminded me that our concession from Lobengula did not confer such powers of government or administration as were mentioned in our charter. He said that these powers would have to be obtained whenever a proper and favourable time for approaching Lobengula on such subjects arrived.

'Jameson's rather broad interpretation of Lobengula's

permission to dig a hole in the east had caused me to assure the High Commissioner that Lobengula had sanctioned our occupation of Mashonaland. On the strength of my assurance, the High Commissioner was prepared to authorize the march of our pioneers. It was therefore extremely important that Lobengula should not upset our plans by sending objections to the High Commissioner. So Jameson returned to Bulawayo to make certain that Lobengula behaved. I will let him carry on from here.'

Jameson took the stand once more. 'I returned to Bulawayo. This time my object was not only to see that the old buster did not throw a spanner into our wheels and upset our apple cart but it was also to explain to him why we needed so many men to dig our hole and why a road had to be cut. When I told him that there would be a hundred wagon-loads of provisions and mining-tools, and a detachment of police to protect the pioneers, he asked, "Against whom are the workers to be protected?" I replied, "Against the Boers, against the Portuguese, against anyone else who might molest them." I am sure he guessed who I meant by "anyone else". I tried to get him to sanction the Pioneers' March and to give the assurance that they would pass unmolested to Mashonaland, but he refused. I felt I was getting nowhere with him, and so decided to leave his country.

'The following day, with my horses saddled, I went to say good-bye to him. The door of his hut was in two portions, an upper and lower one. The upper one was opened, the other closed. Leaning over the closed portion, I saw Lobengula for the last time. He was almost naked and rather agitated. He was pacing to and fro the walls of his badly lit little hut. "Well, king," I said, "as you will not confirm your promise and grant me the road, I shall bring my white impi, and if necessary we will fight." Lobengula replied, "I never refused the road to you and your impi." "Very well," I replied, "then you acknowledge that you have promised to grant me the road and unless you refuse now, that promise holds good." The king said nothing. And while he maintained this diplomatic silence I said, "Good-bye, chief, you have given your promise about the road and on the strength of that promise I shall bring in my impi to Mashonaland." I jumped on my horse and left.

'I never saw him again. In spite of everything I felt sorry for him and considered it a pity that we could not get our way without destroying him.'

Rhodes went on, 'On 6 June 1890 the British High Commissioner informed me that having carefully considered the political position he now considered that the time had arrived for him to give his consent to the entry of the Company's forces into Mashonaland by the route already agreed upon, that is to say, by a route that would skirt Matebeleland proper and leave all Matebele kraals to the north and west of the expeditionary force. He emphasized that the object to be attained was a peaceful occupation of Mashonaland and that it was desirable that all officers should be instructed to be most careful and prudent in the treatment of the natives and to respect their prejudices and susceptibilities.

'I was delighted with this news. My next problem was how to select, organize, and transport my pioneers to Mashonaland.'

Rev. Rhodes asked, 'You never informed the High Commissioner, did you, that Lobengula had not sanctioned your occupation of the country?'

'No, we never told him that but in actual fact it did not matter. He had compelling reasons of his own, such as the rumours of a Boer expedition into the country, to want to see us move in with or without Lobengula's permission.'

'If that is the case, why did you ever seek Lobengula's permission?'

'We merely wanted to avoid fighting. We had long decided to enter Mashonaland whether Lobengula liked it or not. But if we could have got him to sanction our entry and thus avoid fighting and consequent loss of life—so much the better. There was also the British public to consider, British public opinion might have reacted badly if we had begun shooting our way into the country and this might have forced the High Commissioner to intervene and prevent us from going any further. When Lobengula would not co-operate we bluffed him into believing that his position was hopeless and ours was unassailable. We took a chance and pulled it off.'

'I see.'

LOBENGULA'S VERSION

At the indaba tree Council of the Amandebele, Lobengula still held the floor.

'It was at this time that uJemisoni came to our country. I was sick when he arrived and he gave me medicine which made me feel well. I was very grateful to him and since he had doctored me, I made him an induna of the Amandebele, because the king's doctor must be an important man in the nation. One day Jemisoni asked me for permission to cut a road into the country. I told him that there was only one road into my land and that is the road which passes through my kraal. I also said that all strangers who enter my country must use that road. He was still talking when I stood up and went to my wives' quarters where he could not follow me. Later I ordered my oxen to be inspanned and drove to the National Shrine. There I met my senior indunas and doctors.

'I was actually offering sacrifices to Mlimu when I noticed

that all the doctors' eyes were staring at something behind me. I turned and was surprised, nay, shocked to see Jemisoni and Doyili walking up to me. I could not utter a word.

'The doctors and indunas, filled with horror and rage at such outrageous, insulting sacrilege, surrounded the whitemen and would have torn them to pieces with their bare hands if I had not told them not to defile their hands with blood of strangers at the time of important sacrifices to Mlimu. Jemisoni then asked, "Is the king's word always to be believed?" and I replied, "The king never tells a lie," and continued to offer my sacrifices. At that moment, one or two of the indunas bundled the whitemen away. They were lucky our custom forbade us to spill blood at that time.

'A few weeks later uSelu, Edwards and Doyili came to see me. I was glad to see them because we all knew them well. Selu told me that he had been sent by Lodzi to make a new road into the country. He asked me to give him men to help him cut trees and said that I had promised Jemisoni that I would provide the whitemen with people to work on this new road.

'I told him that I had never given Jemisoni any such promise and would not allow a new road to be built. I repeated that there was only one road into my country and that was the one which passed through Bulawayo and said that if Lodzi wanted to send his men round my country let him send them by sea beyond the Sabi River.

'I also told him that Lodzi had sent many people to me all claiming to be his mouth but the words of these mouths of his did not agree. Today one says this, tomorrow another says that, and the following day yet another mouth not only says a different thing but also tells people that I told him things I never said. I told these men that I was sick and tired of talking to Lodzi's mouths and asked why Lodzi was afraid of coming to see me himself.

'I told Selu and his friends to go back to their home, find Lodzi, take him by the hand and bring him here, to me, so that I can speak to him face to face and settle this matter very quickly.

'Doyili replied and said that Lodzi was a very busy man and would not find the time to come so far to my country and also suggested that even if Lodzi came to Bulawayo, no one could say when he would be able to see me because it was not easy for people to see me.

'I told him that he could tell Lodzi that the issues between us could all be settled on the day following his arrival here and he could return to his home on the third day.

'The whitemen then left saying that they were going to bring Lodzi. I never saw Lodzi and these men never returned to see me again.'

Then Mzilikazi said, 'Can you tell us something about the rifles? Did you ever receive any large number of rifles from Jemisoni?'

'No, I never received any large number of rifles.'

'The whitemen say that they gave you 500 rifles and 500,000 rounds of ammunition.'

'I never received any such quantity of rifles. If I had received them, don't you think that we would have used them to prevent the whiteman's entry into the country or even in the war that followed? Why is it that we continued to fight the whitemen with spears? We had no guns.'

The indunas chorused, 'We had no guns. We would have finished them if we had been armed with guns.'

CHAPTER NINE

The 1890 Invaders

Rhodes continued his story. 'For a number of days I tried to solve the problem of selecting, organizing and transporting my pioneers to Mashonaland without success. It appeared as if the whole operation would have to be delayed until the Chartered Company had sufficient funds to meet the expense involved. But time was not on my side. I had to make a move into Mashonaland that winter. Lobengula's refusal to co-operate and give his word that the pioneers would not be interfered with compelled me, however, to provide a protective force strong enough to stand up to the Matebele. I ultimately solved the problem by giving Frank Johnson a contract to do the job. Frank Johnson is here, I will let him tell you how this happened.'

Frank Johnson rose and walked to the altar rails and began. 'Early in the morning of 22 December 1889, I arrived in Kimberley by post-cart from the interior. Kimberley was then a "railhead" and the one train on each alternate day left at night, so I had over a day to spend there on my way back to the Cape. I breakfasted at the Kimberley Club. Outside the summer heat lay heavy on the town. A few minutes later Rhodes entered the room. He looked vaguely at me, and then suddenly recollecting me, silently sat down at my table. He gave an order for bacon and eggs, and then, in his downright, direct and inimitable way, he plunged without preamble into the story of his troubles and asked for my opinion.

'Rhodes said that up to this time he had been unable to find any practical way of taking possession of the country for which he had the charter. At first, he had thought of obtaining from the Imperial Government a force of regular troops who, at one shilling a day, would be five times as cheap as any colonial force; the occupation of Mashonaland being, of course, impossible without a sufficient protective force, on account of the Matebele.

'When this scheme proved impossible he was advised to apply to Major-General (then Colonel) Sir Frederick Carrington, commanding the Bechuanaland Border Police, for advice on the military problem of the occupation of Mashonaland.

'Sir Frederick, Rhodes told me in sentences in which anger and surprise struggled with despair, had laid it down that a minimum of 2,500 men would be required. Such a force (the privates drawing colonial rates of pay—five shillings a day—and free rations), to say nothing of the capital cost of horses and transport, would in the most favourable circumstances, have cost something like a million sterling.

' "Our whole paid-up capital," said Rhodes, "is only £250,000, and out of that I have undertaken to build a railway to Mafeking."

'He leaned his elbow on the table, frowning heavily. "And we can't afford to fail," he went on. "If we send a weak expedition, it will mean disaster. Then the whole Chartered Company will be ruined."

'He shook his head despondently and went on eating. At that time, there was only one known road, or rather track, into the country—the so-called "trade route", running roughly due north from Kimberley through Bechuanaland

and the Bamangwato Country to Matebeleland, a distance of about eight hundred miles, and then north-east to the Mashona country, another three hundred miles. I gathered that this was considered the one possible and practical route. But it involved passing, or more probably forcing, a way through the heart of Matebeleland, where Lobengula could most probably put 30,000 trained warriors in the field, and so I was inclined to think that Carrington, lacking knowledge of the country and people beyond the Bechuanaland Protectorate, had made his estimate in an optimistic mood. Probably not more than a dozen Englishmen knew Mashonaland in those days, and of these I think I was the only one with any previous military training. Hence, I suppose, Rhodes' appeal for my opinion.

'Purely from a desire to cheer Rhodes up, I suddenly broke in: "Two thousand five hundred men is absurd." Then, wishing to emphasize my statement, I added rashly: "Why! with 250 men I would walk through the country!" Rhodes, I remember, lapsed into silence and kept his eyes on his plate, as though he had not heard me, while I—I also remember—went on eating eggs and bacon. For quite a minute nothing was said.

' "Do you mean that?"

'Remember, I had not given five minutes to the problem —my one idea had been to cheer up a worried man, and I might just as easily have said twenty-five men as 250. I had merely blurted out the first divisible of Carrington's figure that came to my head. However, I was not going to plead guilty to having said something I did not mean. I answered at once, "Of course I do." Another long characteristic pause while he rapidly calculated—and then out came the practical businessman.

' "How much will it cost?" he asked. "I have not the slightest idea," I replied. "But give me the use of a room and plenty of paper and by lunch-time I will let you know."

'"Right," was Rhodes' laconic decision. During the next four hours I sat behind locked doors hard at it organizing on paper the future Pioneer Corps, settling its establishment, rates of pay, calculating the pay-roll for a month, the cost and weight of food, etc., etc., etc. Suddenly confronted with the problem of the occupation of Mashona country, a very brief "appreciation of the situation" determined me to wipe out any idea of an advance along the existing trade route through the heart of Matebele country. Had I been a regular soldier looking for "trouble", with its consequent record of war services and a possible D.S.O., I should, of course, have gone via Bulawayo, but with the force I had let myself in for this was out of the question. Somehow the Matebele had to be given a miss. I considered that an expedition on the modest scale I was contemplating could only succeed if it traversed the "low country" along the left bank of the Limpopo, got well to the eastward of the occupied part of Matebeleland and then swung north-east towards the high veld of Mashonaland.

'I estimated the force would require a month to reach some advanced base on the Limpopo in Khama's country, and another four months in which to cut a road through nearly four hundred miles of country mostly thickly wooded and traversed at right angles by a number of big rivers flowing south into the Limpopo. Through all this country no wheeled traffic had ever gone before. It was devoid, in the main, of population, and entirely of tracks and little or nothing was known of it. I allowed an extra month for possible opposition and another month to cover demobilization and the creation of a civil government: seven months in all. When reckoning the rations, I added a further twelve months' half-rations of Boer meal and full rations of sugar, salt, tea and coffee, in case the little settlement should be cut off from the outer world during the following season by impassable rivers or by the Matebele.

'Now and then I would stop my calculations to stare through the windows of the room in which I was sitting, over the tin roofs of Kimberley, and in my imagination I seemed to see beyond an expedition taking living shape. I saw a small band of 250 men with their 117 ox wagons and horses winding laboriously through the African bush. But at that moment these dreams were just so many figures on sheets of foolscap.

'At last I finished working out the figures and then added a fair percentage of profit. The total sum amounted to £87,500 (subsequently increased to £90,400). Before going back to the club for lunch, and well within the four hours I had requested, I was able to lay my figures before Rhodes.

' "There you are," I said, "I have worked the whole thing out and these are my figures." Rhodes studied my sheets, occasionally muttering figures aloud: "One hundred and seventy-nine pioneers—a hundred and fifty natives—£30,000 advance." For about fifteen minutes Rhodes was a changed man and became as optimistic and full of good spirits as a schoolboy. Detail was never his strong point, but he could follow it closely enough to see at a glance that, from his point of view, there was, broadly speaking, nothing materially wrong with my estimates. I say from his point of view, because even a twenty-five per cent margin of error would have been nothing to him financially.

'Then he looked straight at me his grey eyes flashing purposefully. "Good! I accept your offer, and you will command the expedition."

'I smiled, but replied, "I am sorry, Mr. Rhodes, I can't do that. You see, I am on my way back to Cape Town. I only worked out these figures for your information, and not to get the job."

' "What?" snapped Rhodes. "You mean to say you refuse to lead the expedition?"

' "Yes," I replied. "As I said, I leave tonight for Cape Town." "Good God, man! Think what you are doing!" Rhodes' face was flushed now with rising temper as he glared at me. "Here I am offering you the chance of your life. The chance to lead those men into a new country, to annex a whole colony." He paced up and down, but I remained silent.

'Of course there was nothing that I could have liked better. It was a job that appealed to me in every point of view. In particular, I had a long reckoning with Lobengula to square up. On the other hand, there were many reasons that made me hesitate, one of which was my pledge to Khama to control personally the prospecting and mineral development of his country. But outweighing all others was one absolutely insuperable objection to my taking service under the British South Africa Company. On its Board were two directors— Lord Gifford and Mr. George Cawston—who had as much reason for disliking me as I had for reciprocating that feeling. No money on earth would, at that time, have induced me to become, even indirectly, a servant of theirs. I told Rhodes so plainly, and he was furious.

' "Why," he pleaded, trying to tempt me from what he considered an unreasonable attitude, "it'll be the biggest thing a man of your age [I was then twenty-three] has done for England since—since the Lord knows when. And you say you want to go back to Cape Town! Bah! I ask you to add a new country to the Empire, and you say—"

' "I leave for Cape Town tonight," was my final reply. Rhodes stared at me, but I was just as determined as he was. For several moments we stood thus, then without a word, Rhodes slammed his battered hat on his head and stamped out of the room.

'After lunch I went to see some friends. I stayed with them till my train left, so I did not see Rhodes again that day. Two days later, I arrived at the Cape.

'On 27 December I received a wire from Rhodes, despatched from a wayside station: "Meet me Cape Town Station on arrival Kimberley train tomorrow." The train arrived on schedule at 7.30 a.m. I saw Rhodes' massive head protruding from a window, looking for me. Relief seemed to light up his features when he saw I had come. Even more impatient than usual, he jumped out before the train had quite stopped. He never even troubled to greet me, beyond saying, "Oh, here you are. Come with me!" Then, leaving his kit with "Tony" (his Cape servant), we walked out of the station.

' "Where can we talk?" asked Rhodes. I suggested Government Avenue at the top of Adderly Street. We jumped into a hansom cab and drove there in silence. I paid the fare, of course, for he was much too occupied to think of trifles, even if he had the cash on him, which I doubt.

'Then began a tramp up and down Government Avenue which I will never forget. It was cool underneath the oak trees. A veil of mist lay on the mountain table, and the fresh scents of early morning rose all around. Rhodes told me he had consulted with Colonial military authorities, who had confirmed Carrington's estimate of the force required and characterized mine as that of a lunatic. Still, Rhodes was good enough to say, instinct told him that I was right and any great force would be a waste of money, even if the sum required had been available. Hence his determination that I should go.

' "Well, do you still refuse to take on the job of commanding my expedition?" he jeered at me. "I am sorry," I replied, "I cannot go, for I have other work to do." For two hours we walked up and down while he tried by persuasion, taunts and every kind of guile to get me to accept the command of the expedition. At last he said: "If you will go, I will get you made a Member for Kimberley." Even that did not tempt me, although Kimberley was a sure seat, being practically a pocket constituency of Rhodes'. Again I refused his offer.

'Rhodes then turned to me, a smile softening his heavy face. "Everybody tells me you are a lunatic," he said, "but I have an instinct you are the right man, and can do it."

'He went on dreamily pointing out the huge mountain looming over us. "Think of the vast hinterland that lies beyond that. A half-continent ruled for the most part by savages. Think of the gold, the farm lands there! Think of the millions starving, huddled together like cattle in the cities at home. We can give them new homes up there, hundreds of acres to live on, instead of one filthy room. We must have that country for the Empire."

'Even then, nothing could induce me to accept service under the Chartered Company as long as the two men in question were on its directorate. Of course I could not help being touched by the compliment. I was naturally extremely keen to prove to my critics that my proposal was not absurd, and I was also genuinely anxious to help Rhodes out of what he said was a difficulty.

'To make a long story short, I finally had a brain-wave and said, "All right, you win. I'll go. But only under one condition. You give me a cheque for £87,500, supply me with field- and machine-guns, rifles and ammunition, and I will undertake to hand Mashonaland over to you fit for civil government within nine months. But I want you to remember that I am not your servant but your contractor."

'For over a hundred yards Rhodes walked on in silence, his hands clasped behind him. He never looked at me or gave any signs of having heard what I had said. Then he stopped suddenly and said: "I will give you that cheque. Now let us go to Poole's and get some breakfast." Thus was the manner of the occupation of Mashonaland decided. During breakfast we talked over plans. Rhodes rushed on with his ideas about men, food, equipment, horses, etc. His master-brain was working out practical dreams. "How much cash will you want?" was his next question. "Thirty thousand will see me through the first stages," I replied. "Right, and you undertake to enlist and equip the pioneers, to make a road, to occupy Mashonaland and hand it over for civil government in nine months' time?" "I do."

'It was agreed that I should at once draft an agreement embodying the details of the contract, based largely on the figures I had given him in Kimberley. I suggested that I should get in touch with a lawyer, but Rhodes refused, saying, "If you are capable of handing over my country to me, you are capable of drawing up an agreement." Two days later I called on Rhodes at the Prime Minister's office with the agreement. At once he put on his hat and without saying a word, marched me off to the offices of the Eastern Telegraph Company. There I met the man who was destined to be my dearest friend until his death—Sir James (then Mr) Siveright, the Commissioner of Crown Lands and Public Works.

' "Siveright, this is Frank Johnson. I have arranged that he shall occupy Mashonaland for me. I've agreed to the terms in principle. He has drawn up a detailed contract which I have no time to read. You go through it and see that it is fair to both of us. When you have settled it, I'll sign it." And with that he turned out of the room as unceremoniously as he had entered it! That evening the contract was signed and credit opened for me at the old Cape of Good Hope Bank for £30,000 on account.

'Early in April 1890, I commenced the concentration of the men who were to form the Pioneer Corps at a spot on the northern bank of the Limpopo. I personally selected the men from literally thousands of applications from all over South Africa.

'After a time Rhodes asked me to limit my recruiting to the sons of leading families in each district of the Cape. "Why?" I asked, and the reply was: "Do you know what will happen to you? You will probably be massacred by the Matebele, or at least we shall one day hear that you have been surrounded and cut off! And who will rescue you do you think? I will tell you—the Imperial Factor (i.e. the British Government). And who do you think will bring pressure to bear on the Imperial Factor and stir them to save you? The influential fathers of your young men." This was Rhodes' idea of "looking ahead" and "taking the long view".

'So when the Corps finally assembled at Camp Cecil, it comprised clergymen, doctors, lawyers (in those days in my ignorance I thought them a necessity to civilized society), farmers, miners, sailors, builders, tailors, butchers, etc.—a complete nucleus of a self-contained civil population.

'The use of military ranks in the Corps made the Governor, Sir Henry Loch, apprehensive, and he enquired from Rhodes what they were for, since the charter only allowed him to supply his mining prospectors with firearms. Rhodes, who had always visualized his pioneers as an armed body of prospectors and farmers, protested his ignorance. "It must be some idea of young Johnson's, but I will see him about it." Sir Henry was, however, not to be put off so easily. I was ordered to appear before him and to offer an explanation. I told him that being up against the great fighting machine of the Matebele it was necessary for our Corps to undergo the strictest military discipline and training. With this view the Governor, himself a soldier, concurred.

'Showing great interest in my plans of organization and preparation, he asked, "What are you going to do about base lines?" "Nothing, sir," I replied, "because there will be none." "What?" cried out Sir Henry. "Did you ever hear of a striking force moving without a base to fall back on, if necessary, and lines of communication?" "No, sir," was my reply. "But might I respectfully ask if your excellency ever heard of a striking force moving with a year's supply of food, ammunition, etc., as I am proposing to do?" Rhodes supported me. I thought we had convinced the Governor, but after a minute he said, "No, Mr. Rhodes, I will not sanction Johnson's force crossing into Matebeleland unless you provide another force of at least four hundred mounted men to hold the base and, if necessary, go to his assistance."

'When we left the Governor, Rhodes was furious and used some very strong language; he nevertheless sent a telegram to Rutherford Harris at Kimberley, instructing him to engage four hundred mounted men at once. This was the birth of the British South Africa Police—still in existence in the country today. It was not until after the B.S.A.P. had been recruited and equipped that Major Pennefather of the Inniskilling Dragoons, then in Natal, was appointed commanding officer with the rank of Lieutenant-Colonel, and of course, senior to myself in military rank. Lieut.-Colonel Pennefather's appointment did, however, present me with a problem. He would be my senior officer and obviously his orders had to be obeyed, even if they were opposed to my own views. Yet, on the other hand, I was not only officer commanding the Pioneer Corps, but I was the man who had contracted to hand over, fit for civil government, a piece of Africa several times the size of England. I decided to write Rhodes a polite note about it. I said that while I had not the slightest ill feeling upon Pennefather's appointment, I would have to hold him responsible for any financial loss I might suffer from being forced to obey my superior officer's orders against my own judgement and wishes.

'Rhodes, who had apparently discussed this matter with the Governor before, arranged another meeting with Sir Henry, at which the three of us discussed the problem. We decided to leave it to the tact and good sense of both Colonel Pennefather and myself. Fortunately, no differences of opinion ever arose between us and we got on excellently the whole time we were working together.

'It had been agreed that I should not only make a road but also build forts separated by three hundred miles from our base at Macloutsie River and Mount Hampden—our destination. We decided that five troops of the Police Force should remain in reserve at the base, while the three remaining troops would accompany us and provide the garrisons for the three forts which were eventually to be known as Victoria, Charter and Salisbury.

'The Pioneer Force was comprised of 196 officers, non-commissioned officers and men. I divided the small force into three troops, one of which was an artillery unit. I had sixteen civilians, including Dr. Jameson, who I found later, had been sent with Rhodes' power of attorney in case Pennefather and I could not agree. Mr. A. R. Colquhoun who had been appointed the first Administrator of Mashonaland, was with us. Selous was our "Intelligence Officer". We also had two Americans—Brown and Orr.

'After an inspection by Colonel Lord Methuen on 23 and 24 June, we left Macloutsie Camp on 26 June and arrived at the Tuli River bordering Matebeleland on 1 July 1890. Here we built our first fort, which was to be our base. Some troops of the B.S.A.P. remained here as a permanent garrison. While at Tuli I also received a visit from several Matebele indunas, who brought a message from Lobengula (written for him by Sam Edwards) in which he asked me what we were doing in "his country". Had the king killed any whitemen that a white impi was collecting on his borders? You have not got the king's "word", it went on, and you must not cross the "Tuli River". To this message I replied that we had the Great White Queen's "word" and this was the bigger word. It was, however, indicated that if we did go on there would be trouble with the king's army. It was even suggested that our whole force was to be wiped out and, in addition, Selous and I were to be skinned alive!

'I decided to settle this matter in a manner which, I thought, would appeal to the native mind. I gave a practical demonstration of our powers by running the searchlight and firing off our nine-pounders and machine-guns. The Matebele indunas were so impressed with this display that they speedily returned to Lobengula with the most startling and hair-raising stories of our "witchcraft". I am certain that the resulting freedom from attack on our journey north was entirely due to this effective demonstration. The native mind will tackle things that can be understood, but when it comes to "witchcraft", then he is mortally afraid. Later, I heard that Lobengula had actually mobilized 20,000 of his army with the intention of stopping us.

'On leaving Tuli, we found ourselves in possible enemy country. Selous went on ahead with the advance guard, cutting the road for the column. This was no easy matter, as our way took us through a country of thick bush, trees and many sandy drifts. Our daily programme on the march was as follows: after we had stood to arms at reveille, patrols were sent out about two miles on either side of the column to make sure there were no Matebele in the vicinity. On their return we next broke laager, advancing about ten to twelve miles to our next camp, which had been prepared the previous day by the advance guard. We used to reach our new camp around 10 a.m., after which we breakfasted.

126

Orderly room followed. The cattle were left outside the laager, our horses within.

'Selous had with him one troop at a time as advance guard acting as protection to the Bamangwato natives, who did the actual work of cutting the road. Other patrols used to go out some ten to fifteen miles on our left and then work back. The natives were under the control of Radicladi, Khama's brother, who proved of great assistance in keeping his men under discipline, as they were inclined to be terrified of being attacked by the Matebele.

'Every night, when the column was halted, the search-light operated, its brilliant beams being directed into the sky and surrounding bush. At intervals I also had electric mines fired. But no shooting was allowed in order not to create any false "alarm".

'On 17 August we went through the "Top of Mgezi Pass". We constructed a fort near by and called it Fort Victoria, leaving Captain Lendy in charge of Troop C of Police for lines of communication duties. We were now on the high veld, where there was less danger of ambush by the Matebele. Later we arrived at Fort Charter and built our last fort of lines of communication. We received news, while here, that the Portuguese were crossing over into the country south-east of us. Colquhoun, accompanied by Selous, left us to visit Chief Mutasa, whom they wanted to prevent from falling into the hands of the Portuguese.

'In the discussions with Rhodes, it had been agreed that I should make a road to the Mashona country. Since we knew no boundaries of this country we agreed that either Hartely Hills or Mount Hampden, which had been identified by the explorer, Baines, should be the objective of our destination. I preferred Mount Hampden, since it was on high veld and well situated between two rivers.

'On 10 September we reached Hunyani late in the

127

afternoon. The whole of the following day we spent crossing the river, since all the 117 wagons had to be double-spanned to go over its steep and difficult banks.

'The next day we broke laager and in a short time came clear of bush at a stream called Makabusi. There we made our camp, to rest oxen and men after the hard work of the previous day. It was while at this spot that I saw, about five miles off, a good-sized kopje. So about midday I rode over to it along with an escort. When I had climbed it with the idea of trying to spot Mount Hampden, I was rewarded by seeing our goal to the north, where it stood out in the surrounding bush country—a great landmark.

'But I saw something else that fascinated me more than Mount Hampden. It was a beautiful open plain with rich red soil, non-swampy, and obviously ideal agricultural land which stretched away from the kopje I was on to the east, to more broken country and was bounded to the south by a stream which would be ideal for a good-sized town. This I thought was an infinitely better site for a capital than the swampy "granite" soil which I remembered surrounded Mount Hampden. Actually, I was not quite right, for I did not then know of a different soil on its south-east side. If I had, the position of Salisbury might have been different.

'Hurrying back to the camp, I found Jameson just finishing his midday meal, and told him of my discovery. I induced him to return with me to the kopje, so that he could see for himself. A few minutes on top of the kopje confirmed my opinion, and he decided, acting for Rhodes, to accept this spot and not Mount Hampden as being the end of my contract. Descending the kopje, we next rode over the ground now covered by the city of Salisbury. Jameson became more and more enthusiastic about the site.

'On 12 September 1890, the column left the camp at Makabusi and rounded the south end of the kopje. Because of a swamp ahead, it wheeled left, round the base of the kopje—Pioneer Street of today—to a position where the swamp ended (Rhodes Avenue now), then, turning half-right, went straight to the position where the Cathedral now stands.

'I selected this particular spot as being well out of range of the kopje, in case it should be occupied by the Matebele, who might for all I knew be following us and at the same time the site was within reasonable distance of the Makabusi River for water. Jameson wanted the civil population to make the town near the laager, but when later I decided to trek back to the corner of the kopje which I considered to be the most suitable site, all men followed me, leaving Jameson and Colquhoun isolated on the other side of the swamp or causeway, as it was later called.

'That night I slept a satisfied sleep—this time as one of the first white men to sleep—as far as I know—on the site of what we named that day Fort Salisbury—in honour of the British Prime Minister of the day. The following day, Saturday, 13 September 1890, at 10 a.m., when those present paraded, all the land claimed by Lobengula as described in the Rudd Concession was annexed to the British Empire. Bisior hoisted the Union Jack, Canon Balfour of the Police offered a prayer, and following a Royal Salute of twenty-one guns, there were three lusty cheers given for the Queen. The men then dispersed for the rest of the day. The following day work started on the building of the fort, for which I had contracted. This was built on the site of what is now Cecil Square, facing the present Parliament House. In this way we took Lobengula's country. It is said that the Mashona saw us hoist the flag. Those of them who guessed what was happening told their elders who simply said, "Regai vatore zvinoera! Let them take that which is so sanctified that it is not to be taken—the consequences will be theirs." '

Rev. Rhodes then said, 'Why did you annex the country to the British Empire? Wasn't that going beyond your instructions since the Chartered Company only had rights to "dig" in Mashonaland?'

'My instructions were to add the territory to the Queen's dominions and that is what I did, sir.'

ATTEMPT TO STOP INVADERS WITH WORDS

At the indaba, Lobengula continued. 'Although the whitemen, Selu, Doyili and Edwards did not return, I knew that an impi was gathering on the Macloutsie River. I wrote to the big induna in Cape Town and said that he should ask the Queen why, when we are joined together, she was sending her impi into my country. Is it not what Joni told me, when he first came and made me sign a piece of paper? Did he not say that the Queen and I would be joined together in friendship and peace and that our impis would not fight one another? Did Helm and Ladi also not say that the Queen would be my friend?

'I told the Queen these words. "Lodzi paid me money for which I gave him a piece of ground to dig. If you have heard that I have given my whole country to Lodzi, it is not my word. It is not true. I have not done so. Lodzi wants to take my country by strength."

'I reminded the Queen that her words to me were that I was to send to her when I was troubled by whitemen. I told her that I was now in trouble and wanted her to help me control these children of hers.

'I received this reply from the Queen. "The Queen assures Lobengula that the men assembled by the British South Africa Company are not assembled for the purpose of attacking him, but on the contrary, are assembled for a peaceful object, namely searching for gold. They were ordered to travel at a distance from the Matebele kraals and always to recollect that Lobengula is the friend of the Queen and that the Queen wishes to maintain peace and friendship with Lobengula." This is the reply I received from the Queen. She spoke words of peace and yet her impi was waiting at my door with guns and bullets.

'I also sent a word to the impi at Macloutsi. I asked them, "Has the King killed any whitemen that an impi is collecting on his border? Or have the whitemen lost anything they are looking for?" The answer I received was that the men were a working party, protected by soldiers who were going to Mashonaland along the road already arranged with me. Since I did not know of any such arrangement I sent another letter to the impi and told them that I had made no agreement with anybody about a road to Mashonaland. I also said that all I knew was that Jameson could dig a hole near Tati and nowhere else. I said that if Jameson had thought that by Tati I meant Mashonaland, he was mistaken.

'The impi replied to me with these words. "The impi must march on because of the orders of the Queen!" But is this not the same Queen who had told me that she was my friend and wanted to live in peace with me?

'I called together all my impis and told them to get ready for war. I ordered them to wait for my word. My impis were very keen to bathe their spears in the blood of the whitemen, but I decided to wait. I did not want to fight. So I let the whitemen go to Mashonaland.

'Some time later, however, Joni came to me and said that I should give Lodzi's men, in Mashonaland, the right to make laws for the whitemen who were there. I told Joni that I did not want to hear anything about Lodzi's men because they had lied to me. I told him that I had never given them the right they claimed to dig all over my country. I had only said that they could dig one hole near Tati.

'I told him that the whitemen should not have gone behind my back and entered my country through the back door. They should have come here first. They should have passed through Bulawayo. I said, now Lodzi wants me to give him power to punish whitemen in Mashonaland. Why should he ask me today? Did I give him power to enter my country? When did we discuss this matter? Who was there? I said, "Did not the Queen say I should not give all my herd of cattle to one man? Now who has got the herd to kill today?" I asked. I refused to hear anything more about Lodzi and his men.'

Mzilikazi interrupted, 'Wait a minute. When you saw the whitemen's impi gathering at Macloutsie you protested to the Queen and asked why she was doing this when you were joined together, that is, allies, is that right?'

'Yes, that is so, my father.'

'Although the Queen told you that these men were assembled for a peaceful purpose and that she wanted to live in peace with you, it was clear to you that these men were, in fact, an impi and not just peaceful travellers.'

'That is so indeed, my father.'

'There was no doubt in your mind what the gathering of an impi at Macloutsie meant, because you told the Queen that Rhodes wanted to take your country "by strength".'

'That is so, my father.'

'Why, then, did you not stand up to Rhodes and prevent him from taking your country by strength? Why did you not fight?'

'I thought that if I appealed to the whitemen's sense of justice and fair play, reminding them how good I had been to them since I had never killed or ill-treated a whiteman, they might hear my word and return to their homes.'

'And when you saw that your words were falling on deaf ears, what did you do?'

'I sent another message and told them that I had not given them the road to Mashonaland.'

'Yes, and they replied and told you that they had been given the road by their Queen and would only return on the orders of their Queen. What did you do then?'

'I mobilized the army and told them to wait for my word.'

'Did you give that word?'

'No.'

'Were the soldiers keen to fight?'

'Yes, they were dying to fight.'

'Why did you not let them fight?'

'I wanted to avoid bloodshed and war.'

'I see. A king of the Amandebele, who was born, bred and lived only to spill blood of men now did not want to spill blood. Was it only the whiteman's blood or all blood that you did not want to spill?'

There was silence.

'You heard my question. Answer me, Lobengula.'

'I did not want to spill whitemen's blood.'

'Why?'

'Because I wanted to be friends with them.'

'Is that so? What did you do to be friends with them?'

'Nothing. I just did not kill them.'

'And you allowed them to flout your word as king of the Amandebele? You let them have their way: march up to Mashonaland after you had told them as king, not to go? Is that right?'

'Yes. Because I knew we could never defeat the whiteman in battle.'

'If that is so, why did you not do something to become their friend? Why did you not, like Khama, seek their protection and declare your country a British Protectorate?'

'I was afraid of the effect such a move would have on my people, particularly the majaha. I knew that they would have opposed it and might have taken up arms against me.'

'So, fear of the majaha or a civil war prevented you from doing what you knew you should have done to save your country.'

'Yes, I knew that if I fought the whitemen I would be beaten. If I sought the whiteman's friendship and protection there would be opposition to me or civil war. So I decided to pretend to the whitemen that if they came into the country I would fight, and hoped that they would be afraid and not come. When they called my bluff and came I decided first to keep quiet.'

'Was there no other way out of your dilemma?'

'I did consider marrying the Queen, but even though I hinted at this several times no one followed it up.'

'I see!'

CHAPTER TEN

Undeclared War

Rhodes again took up the narrative in the English church. 'It is not necessary for me to say how delighted we all were with the success of the march of the Pioneer Column. Indeed, when their safe arrival in Mashonaland, without incident or loss of life was reported to me, I felt that my life had been worth living. I had looked at this part of Africa and had said, "This earth shall be English," and now it was English.

'For two years we were on the friendliest of terms with Lobengula who looked forward to receiving, each month, the globular sum of £100 in gold sovereigns, which we paid him in accordance with the terms of our concession. I was therefore not prepared for the news I received from Jameson one day when he reported that trouble was brewing between Lobengula and ourselves in the Fort Victoria district. I will let Jameson tell you, himself, what happened.'

Jameson once more walked up and took the stand at the altar rails. 'Although we lived in peace with Lobengula for close on two years,' he said, 'things were not always easy. The Matebele were parasites of the Mashona. They rarely produced enough food in their fields to support themselves. Their country was not suitable for growing such crops as they depended upon for their day-to-day food. So they exacted tribute in grain and cattle from Mashona chiefs. This tribute was collected by parties of armed bands. If a chief resisted, the armed bands formed an impi and descended upon him like a plague of locusts destroying and sacking his villages, looting his grain and cattle and killing all the men, women and children in the area. Furthermore, some Mashona chiefs were given royal herds to pasture and when these were lost or stolen an impi was sent to destroy the village where the theft had occurred.

'Several such impis were sent in areas where the settlers were trying to farm or mine. These raids created a problem for us because they unsettled our labourers and since we could not do anything to stop them, our Mashona servants soon thought that the Matebele were more powerful than white men. In April 1893, five hundred yards of our telegraph wire were stolen. No trace of the wire could be found. We induced a Mashona named Gomala to admit the theft and then impounded his cattle. What we did not know was that these cattle belonged to Lobengula. Gomala reported this to the king who was, naturally, very annoyed with us. I immediately informed him that the cattle would be returned. In spite of this assurance, Lobengula decided to send an impi to punish Gomala for having acquiesced to our taking the king's cattle from him.

'First he sent a small impi which was turned back by Captain Lendy at Fort Victoria. Then he sent a large impi under an elderly induna, Manyowu, and a younger man called Mgandana. He, however, sent a letter to Captain Lendy and another one to me, assuring us that the impi would not harm any white men.

'The impi went straight to Fort Victoria, where white men suddenly saw hundreds of Mashona flocking to the settlement shouting *Hokoyo, bayo Madzviti!* Beware there come the Matebele! Some whitemen rode out and indeed saw hordes of Matebele warriors armed with spears, shields and one or two guns. They went to the induna who told them that they were hunting Mashonas to kill them for stealing the king's cattle. By this time other Matebele had already entered the township and were pursuing and stabbing to death any Mashona they saw. Parties of white men under Captain Lendy then rode out to rescue white men's cattle that were being driven away. Many Mashonas had, at this time, taken to the hills and the plumed Matebele were in hot pursuit.

'We later counted over four hundred Mashona men, women and children slaughtered in this way. The roads and surrounding bushes were strewn with dead bodies. Although the Matebele had not killed any white men they had killed their Mashona servants before their eyes, had mutilated and cut the throats of their sheep, goats, dogs, cats, and chickens. Several Matebele had shouted to white men, "We will not touch you today, but your day is coming, white dogs."

'I received the news of these events in Salisbury, a day after they had taken place. I also received, at the same time, Lobengula's reassuring letter. I therefore sent the following message to Captain Lendy:

Have you heard of the king's message to me? You will see he is very anxious and in fact frightened of any trouble with whites. But you have done absolutely right in taking all precautions. What you should do now is this: see the head induna as soon as possible. Tell him of the king's message and my reply, and if necessary, that you would act up to it with police, volunteers and your machine-guns. At the same time, remember the excessive importance of not hinting at this if avoidable. From a financial point of view it would throw the country back till God knows when. In short, you have authority to use extreme measures if necessary; but I trust you to use tact to get rid of the Matebele without any actual collision.

'I also sent the following message to Lobengula:

I thank the king for his friendly message. I have nothing, of course, to do with his punishing his own Moholis. But I must insist that his impis be not allowed to cross the border agreed upon by us. He not being there, they are not under control and Captain Lendy tells me that some of them have actually been in the streets of Victoria, burning kraals within a few miles and killing some Mashonas who are servants of the white men. I am now instructing Captain Lendy to see the head induna and tell him the cattle must be returned at once. His impi must retire beyond our agreed border; otherwise he is to take his police and at once expel them, however many there are. The king will see the necessity of this, otherwise it is possible, the white men getting irritated, his expedition may never return to Bulawayo.

'The following day I decided to go to Fort Victoria and so telegraphed Lendy to keep the induna there till my arrival.

'While I was travelling to Fort Victoria about a dozen Matebele led by Manyowu came to the township and presented Lobengula's letter to Captain Lendy. When asked why they did not deliver the letter when they first arrived, they said that the man who carried the letter had a thorn in his foot and could not walk fast. They asked that the Mashona in the town be given up to be slaughtered. Manyowu said, "I will not kill them here and dirty your place. I will take them to the bush, yonder, and kill them there." Lendy replied that if Manyowu had any charges to

138

lay against any Mashona present, he would, as Magistrate, hear them, but he would not surrender all and sundry to be summarily executed. Manyowu then declared that all the Mashona belonged to the king and considered it grossly unfair for white men to refuse to give them up, whereas the king always gave them up to the white men when the latter wanted to punish them.

'We could see, as we drove near Fort Victoria, hundreds of Mashona kraals burning on all sides. Some Mashonas came to speak to us when we outspanned. But, seeing the Matebele about two miles away, they rushed to the hills for refuge, leaving one of their prettiest girls near by with a calabash of food.

'When I arrived in Fort Victoria, the whole township was in a laager. The Rev. Sylvester had just completed a sermon preached from a pulpit of an ammunition case, in which he called upon the Lord to clear out the sons of Ham. The settlers asked me what protection they would have from the Matebele and demanded a showdown which would eliminate the Matebele menace once and for all.

'I asked the Matebele indunas to meet me. Two to three hundred men came towards us, but we allowed only a few unarmed indunas to come as far as the fort.

' "What do you mean by coming here and doing what you have done?" I asked.

' "I was sent by the king to punish the Mashonas for stealing the king's cattle," Manyowu replied.

' "The king never told you to do that, because I have a letter from him," I said.

' "I have told you the king's orders to me," Manyowu insisted.

' "You lie," I said.

'Then Mgandana, trembling with anger, said, "How can you insult us by telling an old man like this that he is lying?

Who do you think you are? I can tear you to pieces now, now, dog of whiteman."

' "I do not talk to boys. I talk to men," I told Mgandana. Several young Matebele men began shouting and gesticulating arrogantly and defiantly. "Is it true that you have no control over your young men?" I asked Manyowu.

' "These are not children but men," the old man replied.

' "Very well," I said, "you go with the older men and I will deal with the younger men. Now go, or I will drive you across," I said.

' "Very well," said Mgandana, "we will be driven across." As he walked away Mgandana said, "We must collect all our impis together tonight and drive these white dogs from here."

'After this, I told Captain Lendy to get fifty mounted men. I said to the men, "You have heard what I told the Matebele. I do not want them to think it was a mere threat. Ride out in the direction they have gone, towards Magomoli's kraal. Drive them as you heard me tell Manyowu I would, and if they resist, you shoot them." A party under Captain Lendy was soon ready to move.

'The impi was taken by surprise. It was scattered about killing and plundering when it heard the white men's bugle and fire. Lendy's party was armed with repeating rifles and with every man a crack shot, the Matebele fell down like bags of mealies. Mgandana, conspicuous in his headdress of beautiful white feathers was seen to stand up, menacingly shake his spear, and drop down dead.

'I must say of Mgandana, however, although I considered him arrogant and insolent, he had plenty of pluck. He was every inch an aristocrat. One of the white men who was present at Fort Victoria said that Mgandana was the most handsome person of African descent he had seen.

'The Matebele impi fled in all directions. The triumphant Lendy's party returned to the laager before sundown.

'After this taste of easy victory it was impossible to prevent the settlers from following up their success and striking at Lobengula before he was ready. I spent that evening telegraphing Rhodes. I told him that I proposed to fight the Matebele. Rhodes replied, "Read Luke xiv, 31." I looked it up in the Bible and read, "Or what king, going to make war against another king, sitteth not down first, and consulteth whether he be able with ten thousand to meet him that cometh against him with twenty thousand."

'I wired back that I had read the verse and it was all right. Rhodes pleaded that the company had no money and he had already spent a considerable amount of his own money on company business. I told him that he must, by hook or crook, find the money. He did.

'I asked Major Forbes to raise an army and assume full command. I promised to pay the men for their services by grants of land and gold claims in Matebeleland. Since it was generally believed at this time that, because Mashonaland had proved to be without gold, the gold lay in Matebeleland, it was not difficult to find recruits.

'The army was soon ready. A column from Salisbury joined the one from Fort Victoria before meeting Lobengula's army at Shangani. Thanks to the fog we were lucky to avoid detection by Lobengula's army in the Filabusi forests, where it lay waiting for us. Thus, when we met it, it was on the plains where conditions were more favourable to us and our guns than to the Matebele, with their spears. Still, it is true to say that at Shangani as well as at Imbembesi, the Matebele impi fought with great courage and bravery. The Imbezu and Ingubu regiments bore the brunt of our thrust and were practically completely annihilated. Sir John Willoughby, an officer of the Guards, who had fought in many battles in the Empire, said of the Matebele warriors—who were on the field that day, "I cannot speak too highly of the pluck of these two regiments. I believe that no civilized troops anywhere in the world could have withstood such terrific fire as we unleashed for even half as long as the Matebele took it. We hit them with everything we had but, hour after hour they kept on coming until they were almost all wiped out. When we reached Bulawayo, the king had set fire to his kraal and fled. Some of a party sent to capture him were annihilated by the Matebele. The king died soon after, however, and our authority in Matebeleland became undisputed."

'That is how we conquered Lobengula. That is how we won Matebeleland.'

'Dr. Jameson, when you decided to march against Lobengula into Matebeleland, did you warn him or send word to him in any way?' asked the Rev. Rhodes.

'No, I did not.'

'So there was no ultimatum of any sort.'

'No, there was not.'

'Was there a declaration of war?'

'No, there was not.'

'So you decided to march in war against a man for whom you had all along professed friendship, without an ultimatum or a formal declaration of war.'

'There was nothing I could do. The whites were all eager to have the matter settled once and for all.'

'What about the Moffat Treaty and all the assurances of peace that your company and British officials had made to Lobengula?'

'We did not think about them at the time.'

'All you thought of was that you had an opportunity to dispose of Lobengula whose impis were more than a nuisance to you and in any case there was the attraction of a rich prize, in the gold and land in his country.'

'Yes.'

'You spoke of Mgandana as having been truculent and insolent. What about you? Don't you think you were insolent, stuck up and swollen-headed?'

The doctor remained silent.

'I think if you had been a little more tactful and courteous it might have helped.'

WHEN THE ASSEGAI BROKE

Lobengula appeared less confident than before as he began to narrate the events which led to the termination of his reign. Members of the Council also appeared subdued and more serious than usual. Perhaps the very close questioning of Lobengula by the Bull Elephant had disturbed their thoughts and cast some doubts on the wisdom of some of his actions. Lobengula spoke as most men sat with their eyes fixed to the ground, and said, 'Now, my father, I must tell of the war. The whiteman's war which brought to an end Amandebele power in our land. It is not a story I am happy to narrate, but tell you I must, since to do otherwise would be to hide behind a finger.

'The war with the whitemen was sparked off by something which had nothing to do with them. I had a large number of cattle which were in the custody of a Mashona chief who lived near the Guruguru hill not far from what is now Pakame Mission in the Selukwe district. Now, there was a man in the Fort Victoria district whose name was Mushandu. Mushandu hired a *gororo*, that is, a professional thief with magical and supernatural powers, to steal my cattle for him. The gororo, whose name was Kupara, travelled to Guruguru at night and cast a spell on the village where my cattle were kept. This spell was carried in a dog's skull lately severed. After he cast his spell on this village, the people of

143

the village slept as if they were dead. He then went to the cattle kraals and drove away my whole herd to Mushandu's village. Two cows separated from the herd, however, and before Kupara had noticed this fact, they had crossed a little stream that was some distance from Mushandu's village. Since crossing a stream would break the spell he had cast on the village where he had stolen the cattle, he left these beasts where they were and drove the rest to Mushandu's kraal.

'On his way, he went past chief Magamure Zimuto's kraal and propitiated the spirits of Zimuto's ancestors by leaving one-fourth of the cattle he had stolen with Zimuto. Before leaving them, however, Kupara took the precaution of changing the colour of these cattle making black ones brown, white or spotted, and white ones black. This he could do because of his supernatural powers and ability to call upon the ancestral spirits of the area to make his spell hold. He told Zimuto that he had left two cows in the forest and asked Zimuto to fetch them.

'He passed on to Mushandu's kraal, where he left half the herd and kept the other half as his fee. When the spell finally broke and the people at Guruguru found that the cattle had disappeared, they followed their trail to Zimuto's kraal. On examining Zimuto's cattle, however, they found none they could recognize as my cattle except two—the two that Kupara had left behind and whose colour he had not changed.

'They returned and reported this to my induna uMgandana. I decided to send a small impi under the command of my indunas uManyowu and Mgandana to punish Zimuto. Not wishing in any way to frighten or harm whitemen, I wrote a letter to the white induna at Fort Victoria and told him that I wished to recover my cattle and punish Zimuto. I advised the white people not to worry because my soldiers had instructions not to touch any whiteman.

'The white induna Lendy, at Fort Victoria, refused to let my impi punish Zimuto and recover my cattle, saying that he was the magistrate to decide whether Zimuto had done any wrong and what punishment should be given him. Furthermore, he told my impi that they should keep on their side of the boundary and leave the whiteman's side alone.

'Now what kind of talking was this? Since when had white men power over my Amahole? Who had appointed Lendy a magistrate to decide cases for me? Who had told the whitemen there was a boundary over which my impis could not cross?

'I decided to be firm. I sent back Manyowu and Mgandana with a much larger impi and with definite instructions to punish Zimuto and bring back my cattle. Nevertheless, once more, I instructed Dawusoni to write a letter to Lendy at Fort Victoria, in which I said, "I am sending an impi there to punish some people who have stolen my cattle. This impi will probably come across whitemen. I ask the whitemen to understand that the impi has nothing whatever to do with them. They should not oppose it and if the people who have committed the offence have taken refuge among whitemen, I ask the whitemen to give them up for punishment."

'I also sent a message to Harris and Jemisoni telling them what I had done.

'But, after my impi led by Manyowu and Mgandana had left, I received word that Zimuto and his people, in fact, no longer had any cattle, because the whitemen had taken all the cattle in that area as compensation for their wire which they allege had been stolen by Gomala—one of Zimuto's people.

'I was mad with rage. I knew that the whitemen had taken these cattle knowing full well that they were mine and that there was no truth whatsoever in the story that their wire had been stolen. Who would want to steal wire? Can you eat it? What can you do with it?

'I sent a letter to Jemisoni asking him why he had taken my cattle. I said, "Did I cut your wire?" Jemisoni replied that he did not know that the cattle were mine and would send them back. The Gavuna at the Cape also wrote saying that he hoped the matter of my cattle that had been taken by whitemen was over.

'I would have considered the matter settled if my induna Manyowu had not arrived and told me what had happened. Let Manyowu tell you, in his own words, what took place at Fort Victoria.'

The old bearded warrior—veteran of many wars, stood up and began with the customary royal salute of '*Bayete! Bayete! Bayete!*—you are the heavens!' To which the councillors lustily responded, and then said, 'My Lord, the Bull Elephant, the Lion uLobengula, and my fathers. What the Lion says is true. I was sent with the brave and gallant uMgandana to go and punish Zimuto and his people and also to bring back the king's cattle which had been stolen. The king gave us strict instructions not to touch or harm any whiteman. We commanded the uMhlahlandlela, the Noseyika and the Nolima regiments. We travelled to Zimuto's village but found all the villages deserted. There were no people or cattle. We found that the people had gone to the whiteman's village. We went there. We asked to speak to the induna. We told him that we had been sent by the king to punish the people of Zimuto for stealing the king's cattle and to recover the stolen cattle.

'The induna told us all to disarm and discuss the matter properly. We disarmed and sat down. We said that we had orders not to touch any whitemen but to kill all Zimuto's men, women and children. We said that we were quite prepared not to kill the Amaholes in the whiteman's village and

146

thus spoil their drinking water, and that we would slaughter them in the forest farther away.

'We were still discussing peacefully when the whitemen fired on us and told us that the Amahole were no longer the property of Lobengula but now belonged to them. Mgandana was shot on the spot, and taken completely by surprise; we were dispersed. Some of us managed to fight our way out of the trouble, but most of us were slaughtered there. I escaped and took the news to the king.' Manyowu sat down. There was silence for a while and then Lobengula continued,

'At this time I received a message from the Gavuna at the Cape. He told me that the impi of Mgandana and Manyowu had ignored my orders and entered the village of whitemen killing the Amahole servants of the white people before the doors of their houses. He said that the whole country was smelling blood, spilt by my impi. And he wanted me to return the whiteman's cattle. This was a naked lie, for if there was any blood smelling, it was the blood of my men treacherously shot at an indaba.

'I sent the following message to the Gavuna at the Cape. "I shall not return any cattle or compensate anybody until Rhodes returns to me all the Amahole and their wives, children, cattle, goats and sheep which were given protection by the Victoria people. Had I known at the time when I sent my impi what I know now, I would have ordered them to capture and loot all they could lay their hands on belonging to the whites as well, in order to compensate myself for the people and their cattle withheld from me."

'I also sent another message to Lodzi and said, "You did not tell me that you had a lot of Amahole cattle hiding with you together with their owners and that when my indunas claimed them from Captain Lendy he refused and told my induna that the Amahole and their cattle did not belong to me any longer and then turned his guns on my people. Are the Amahole yours? I thought you came to dig gold but it seems that you have come to rob me of my people and country as well. You are like a child playing with a sharp and dangerous knife. Your induna Lendy has no holes in his ears and cannot hear. He is young and foolish and all he thinks of is fighting. You better warn him before it is too late."

'I also sent another message to Jamisoni. I said, "You talk of a boundary between us. Who gave you the lines? Let him come forward and show me the man that pointed out these boundaries." Jemisoni answered and said, "The king knows that ever since we have been here, the Umnyati and Shashi rivers formed the boundaries across which we would not allow our white people to go." But I had never said that my country now ended on the Shashi and the Umnyati rivers.

'I recalled the impi which was on its way across the Zambezi to Barotseland. I said that they should come back at once. The whitemen brought their regular monthly pay of one hundred pounds to me and I refused it. I told them from now onward I did not want it since it was because of this money that they were acting as if I sold them my country.

'I again sent uMtshede to England to go and see the Queen herself, and find out why she was doing all this when we are joined together. But Gavuna at the Cape refused to give him the road because he said Mtshede would not agree to talk about a boundary between me and the whitemen, and he also refused to say that the Amahole did not belong to me. Mtshede said, "If the Amahole do not belong to the king, to whom do they belong?" Gavuna said that my impis were already advancing on the whitemen in Mashonaland. Mtshede told him that all the impis were at home and he could send someone to see for himself.

'Gavuna then sent me a friendly message saying, "My

friend Lobengula, I hear that your impis have fired on white men twice. Be wise, keep your impis away from the white people and send some of your chief indunas to talk to me."

'I agreed to do this and asked my brother Ingubugobo and two indunas to go to Cape Town with Dawson as their guide. I gave them a message to tell Gavuna and my message was: "I am tired of hearing the lies which come to me every day. How many of your people have my people killed? You say my people have fired on yours twice. How many are dead? Are your people stones that the bullets do not kill them? You hear what your people say. Send two men of yours and I will give them assistance to find out who has done this shooting. It is clear that your people want something from me. When you have made up your mind to do something it is not right to blame it on my people."

'When my brother and the indunas arrived at Tati, however, they were arrested by the whitemen. The indunas were killed and my brother was lucky to escape with his life. When I heard this I was very angry indeed. How could Gavuna ask me to send men to discuss matters with him and when I send my men he arrests and kills them? What could one do with such men?

'I then received word, at this time, to the effect that an impi of whitemen, sent by Jemisoni was marching to Bulawayo fully armed. Then I saw what the whitemen were trying to do. The Gavuna was trying to keep me talking peace while his brother Jemisoni came to stab me from behind. These whitemen are indeed fathers of lies. I ordered my army to assemble in front of my kraal and when I came out of my hut I had paint on my face and carried an assegai in my hand. I drove the assegai into the earth with such force that the handle broke. It was war, and that night my impis went out to meet the invading enemy. Please notice that my impis went out, not to attack anyone, but to defend our land. Our country was being invaded; we had to defend it like men, and like men we did our duty, fought and died.

'Of the fighting that took place, I do not wish to speak. Only this, I must say, that in any age, in any land, of any men, where brave deeds are sung or told; the feats of the Amandebele on yonder plain, o'er Shangani and Mbembezi rivers, will for ever shine and glitter with the brightest and best.'

Tears rolled down the Great Lion's cheeks. On the Council silence reigned and reigned supreme. And yet they spoke, but not with their mouths; saw, but not with their eyes; heard, but not with their ears.

It was left to Mtjana, the commander of the Mbizo regiment, to complete the sad story. 'When the news of the defeat of our impi in spite of its heroic stand reached the king, he was not surprised. He appeared to have expected it, because it was a bad omen that the assegai that he threw into the earth to declare war had broken its shaft. Although he knew that the end was near he was calm, cool and collected as he manfully directed the destruction of his capital, Bulawayo. One of the last things he did in this city was to call Sekulu, a chief who lived in the Bulawayo area, and to charge him, upon his life, with the safety of two whitemen —the traders Fairbairn and Usher. These three men remained in the town and saw flames of fire leap up and destroy it completely.

'When the white soldiers were only a few miles away, Sekulu placed gunpowder in the king's hut and blew it up. Then he said to Usher and Fairbairn, "Whitemen, I have done my duty, as a man is bound to do, and carried out the orders of my king. But now I must leave you and go because if your soldiers find me here they will not show me the mercy with which my king has treated you. They will slay me. If anything happens to you now it will be the fault of your people and not of the Amandebele." And he left. The king, attended by the Great Induna uMagwegwe, went in the direction of the Shangani river with Sivalo and Sihuluhulu forming the royal bodyguard. Luthuli and I commanded the regiments that covered the king's retreat.

'We crossed the Shangani and camped on the Gwampa River for the night. The following morning the spoor of the whitemen who were pursuing Lobengula was seen, and our young men, thirsting and yearning for a fight forced us to give chase to them. We did.

'The whitemen had by this time reached Shangani and camped some distance away from the road for fear of being seen by us, for they knew that we would follow. They then sent a small patrol to the king's wagons, and not finding the king there, the little patrol returned to the main group.

'But the king had seen them. He said, "I know they are following me because of this money I have. I know that money is what they want. Sivalo and Sihuluhulu, take this bag of money and give it to the whitemen, perhaps they will return and leave me alone." Sivalo and Sihuluhulu took to the whitemen the bag full of about 1,000 gold sovereigns, which Lodzi had been paying Lobengula every month.

'The whitemen returned to the wagons later. This upset Lobengula, who was heard to say, "But what do they still want? I gave them the money. Why did they take it if they still want to fight?" This time the whitemen left a letter from Jemisoni. In it Jemisoni said that the king should return to Bulawayo and promised him safety and friendly treatment. But Jemisoni also said that the king would be pursued if he did not return.

'Lobengula then told a coloured man named John Jacob who was with him to reply to Jemisoni and say, "It is all right, I will come, but where are the indunas I sent with my brother on a peace mission at the invitation of your Gavuna at the Cape? What happened to them? If I come, where will I live in Bulawayo? My houses have burnt down." Then Jacobs wrote words of his own and said, "Please be so kind and send me ink and pens and paper."

'By this time, the impi had arrived and attacked the whitemen. They sent two of them back across the Shangani River. One rode a white horse and another a brown one with a star on its forehead.

'That night, I lined the road with my impi and cut off the retreat of the whitemen. I sent back to the Shangani River the Isiziba and the Hlati regiments in order to keep back the machine-guns.

'The next day we surrounded the whitemen, but two of them boldly charged through our ranks, and with their horses swam across the flooded river. We attacked those that remained. Mdlilizelwa was the first man to kill a whiteman that day. Bayana was the second, but he was later killed himself. We heard the whitemen sing, but we continued to attack them until we had completely wiped all of them out.

'Lobengula then summoned us and spoke these words. "I thank you for your bravery and for all you have done. You have indeed fought like men.

> In any age, in any land; of any men
> Where brave deeds are sung or told
> The feats of the Amandebele on yonder plain
> O'er Shangani and Mbembezi rivers
> Will for ever shine and glitter
> With the brightest and best.

As for me, I shall disappear like a needle in the grass. No whiteman will ever lay his hands on me, for I do not wish that a single bone or a single hair of mine should ever be touched by white hands. All the people, black and white,

rich and poor, the soil, grass, rivers, hills, rocks, trees, cattle
and dogs, will remember me.

> *Lisale kuhle bantwa bami*
> Fare ye well, my children.
> *Namhla ilizwe lifile*
> Today the world has come to an end."

'And, so saying, he mounted on his pitch-black horse,
while all the warriors around roared *"Bayete! Bayete! Bayete!
Bayete!"* in salute to him for the last time and the women
beat their breasts and wailed in sorrow, crying *"Maibabo,
Maibabo, Maibabo! Intaba yo dilika bantu!"* He rode alone into
the wilderness and disappeared, as he had said, like a needle
in the grass.

'There is a grave that men say is the king's grave, but
those who know shake their heads and whisper that it is the
grave of his great induna uMagwegwe who, like a true noble-
man, vowed to die with his king and consented to be buried
alive in a cave, like a king, so that Lobengula's last wish,
that no whiteman should ever know his grave or touch with
white hands, a single bone, or a single hair of his body,
would be fulfilled for generations and generations to come.'

CHAPTER ELEVEN

In the Bosom of the Spirits

The stage was set for the final act of the drama, at both the Great indaba tree Council of the Amandebele Nation and the congregation at Bishop's Stortford Church, in England. At the former, Lobengula, last of the Amandebele kings had, before his father on earth, told how and why he had lost a kingdom; at the latter, Rhodes, the first white ruler of the country had, in the house of his Father in Heaven declared before his father on earth why and how he had taken that kingdom. Both men stood to be judged, found guilty and sentenced or acquitted according to the code of ethics and conduct of the society in which they had been nurtured and brought up.

The atmosphere was charged with excitement and expectancy. At last the riddle was to be unravelled. Did Lobengula sell out or was he a victim of unscrupulous men? Did he understand what was going on or did he not? Was he a weak or a strong man? Did he lose his kingdom because of some weakness inherent in his character? Was he scrupulous or unscrupulous? Should he have been more scrupulous in dealing with his equally unscrupulous adversary? Would he have saved his kingdom if he had joined them when he realized he could not beat them? Did Lobengula have two sets of ethical standards; one which he applied as an individual—a man—and another as king of the Amandebele? One which he applied in his man-to-man dealings and another in his state-to-state dealings? One which he applied to white men and another to black men?

And Rhodes! Was he scrupulous, fair, honest and straightforward in his dealings with Lobengula or did the end justify any means, as far as he was concerned? What motivated him? Was it self-glorification, love of money, power, or love of mankind? Which mankind? Whites or blacks? British, or just white men? Did the end justify his means? Is the end justifiable as far as Africans are concerned and as far as white men are concerned? What of the future?

Will men consider themselves indebted to Rhodes for a thousand years to come, as he once said, or will they curse him for that long? And Lobengula? What will men think of him in a thousand years? Who really won in Matebeleland?

These questions and many more were soon to be answered. I felt honoured, that I, Gobinsimbi Dabulamanzi Khumalo, would be among the men to hear the spirits in Africa and England pronounce judgement on the conduct of affairs in our land. I was at the Great Council of the Amandebele. Any moment now the Bull Elephant uMzilikazi would call the Council to order and begin answering the questions I have posed. Then I caught the eye of Mncumbata, the mouth, eyes and ears of Mzilikazi. 'Hau! Gobinsimbi, are you here?' he said. 'Yes, I am here, my father, I have been here since the indaba began,' I replied. 'So you have not been here long, then?' he said, apparently glad that I was only a new arrival in the Spirit world. 'Yes, my father, I am but lately come and even the tears are not yet dry on the cheeks of those that mourn me,' I replied. 'That is good indeed,' Mncumbata said, 'for we want you to return—return to the children yonder and tell those that have ears to hear that which you have seen and heard; for your eyes and ears have been open. Now, go, go back to the living, son of Khumalo, go, go and tell what you have seen.'

'But, my father,' I protested, 'the verdict will be delivered soon, both here and at the other place. Can't I remain only long enough to hear its nature and import and then hasten to do as my father commands?'

'No, my son,' he said, 'you will not be able to return to the living if you stay here longer. Even as I speak, you may be late already. No, you will just make it—farewell!'

So I returned to tell my tale. Perhaps it was not the wish of the Spirits that men—mortal men—should know of the judgements, verdicts and sentences that they passed on one another. We shall never know for certain, until we join their number. But those that come to take me are approaching. Soon, I will once more be of their number and will know.

*

Something I do not know or understand seemed to happen to Gobinsimbi, the son of Khumalo, whom men now call Mafavuke. His face grew more gentle and his eyes began to glow. He seemed to be communicating in a way or voice I could not hear, with Beings whose presence I could not feel or see.

Wishing to learn more of the verdict, I said, 'My father Khumalo is a wise man. His eyes and ears have seen and heard that which has never been seen or heard by any living man. Perhaps my father can tell us what he thinks was the verdict on these two men.'

'The verdict, Ngwenya, is in the bosom of the Spirits,' his voice, growing faint, Gobinsimbi continued, 'there it must remain concealed from living men. It is fruitless for men to guess, surmise, and speculate on matters of the Hereafter, for as long as men are living men, and Spirits are dead men who live in the Hereafter, there will always be a barrier separating one from the other which can only be crossed by death. The messengers are here. My time is come. I must now go to join my ancestors. *Sala kuhle Ngwenya, Inkosi ikubusise, mntakaMfundisi. Ubatshele, ukuze, abalendlebe bazwe. Sala kuhle m'taka Samkange.*' Normally, I should have been frightened to see a man dying in front of me and the fact that I was alone with him in the hills would have made me even more scared. But somehow I was not frightened by the death of Gobinsimbi Khumalo. His was not a death but a journey—a journey to a place he had already seen. He was not afraid to die—he was looking forward to it.

I put my arm around him, and holding his hand, said, '*Ngiyabonga Khumalo. Indlela'nhle baba wami. Ngizaba-tshela ukuze abalendlebe bazwe Khumalo! Usikhonzele pham-bili!*' And Gobinsimbi Khumalo departed to the Spirit world in my arms. I laid his body gently on the soft grass at the mouth of the cave, for my heart within me was heavy. I had already become fond of the man. Now that he was gone, what was I to do? I could not bury him alone, I must inform his people. But who were his people? Perhaps I could find out! I remembered what years before, as a Pathfinder at Waddilove Mission, I had been told to do if I suddenly found a dead man in the forest. 'Do not touch him or go near him,' the troop leader used to say, 'but run as fast as you can and report to the police.' So I went straight to my car. And believe me, I only turned the key and the engine started to run as if I had never had any trouble with it the previous day. I drove to the police station. I made my report.

An hour later, I was sitting in a police Land Rover with five constables. We carried a coffin with us. I was directing them to the cave. But a strange thing had happened. The cave and road had disappeared. We could not even find the spot where I had left my car the previous day. With the police, I spent three hours searching high and low for that cave and road and could find neither. I have never been more embarrassed or felt more stupid in my life.

The two white constables, I could see, began to suspect that there might be something the matter with me and that perhaps I was not all there, that is, all right in the head. But several men in that neighbourhood swore by the names of their fathers that they knew a man called Gobinsimbi Khumalo who had died and then returned from the dead. But they did not know what had happened to him, for it seemed, he had just disappeared.

The African sergeant clearly thought he understood what was happening. 'Ah, no, Mr. Samkange. Do not worry,' he said, 'Gobinsimbi Khumalo does not want to be mourned a second time, and so he is preventing us from finding his body.' We gave up the search for that cave.

But if one day, while on the Matopo hills, you find a cave, at the mouth of which a fire once burned, tread reverently on that ground, for it is the ground on which Gobinsimbi the son of Dabulamanzi of the house of Khumalo, whom men called Mafavuke, told his tale to Ngwenya, the son of Samkange of the people of Gushungo. And, who knows, his Spirit may be visiting the cave with you that day.

Glossary of Names and Terms

Abelungu: white man.

Aborigines' Protection Society: a London-based society for the protection of the interests of Africans

Amahole: members of tribes conquered by and considered to be slaves of the Amandebele

Amandebele: name given to Mzilikazi's people by the Basutho people when they passed through the Transvaal

Amangisi: refers to the English

Amaputukezi: Portuguese

Bamangwato: one of the Bechuana tribes under Khama

Barotseland: land occupied by Lozi people across the Zambezi river

Basuto, Basutoland: Sutho-speaking people under Moshoe rule

Bechuana, Bechuanaland: land occupied by a group of Sechuana-speaking tribes (see map)

Bayete: the royal salute of the Amandebele

Bechu: skin apron

British South Africa Police: name of the Rhodesian Police

Bulawayo, Gubulawayo: Lobengula's capital city and largest city in the Matebeleland region of Rhodesia

Bundu: the bush

Bushman: a race of little men who are now found mainly in the Kalahari desert

Chaminuka: a seer who lived a few miles from the present site of the city of Salisbury

Chartered Company: the British South Africa Company which was formed by Cecil J. Rhodes to exercise rights granted by Lobengula in the Rudd Concession. It received a charter from the queen

Chikaka: the main village in the Zwimba Reserve near Sinoia

Doyili: Doyle

Gushungo: clan name of the Zwimba people

Hope Fountain: mission station established by missionaries of the London Missionary Society a few miles from Bulawayo

Hunyani: a river a few miles away from Salisbury

Imboyi: one of the Matebele regiments

Impi: an army

Indaba: literally means a matter; refers to a council or a discussion

Induna: literally means a leader; refers to a commander of a regiment or a chief of a village or tribe

Intab' ezindunda: a hill a few miles from Bulawayo where Mzilikazi executed

Inyati: first mission station established by missionaries of the London Missionary Society

Jani: Viljoen, a prominent Boer

Jemisoni: Dr. L. S. Jameson

Jeni: Moffat

Khama: king of the Bamangwato people of the Bechuana tribes

Kopje: a little hill; refers to the hill near which Salisbury was built

Ladi: Rudd

Lodzi: Rhodes (because the Matebele do not have the letter *r* in their language his name was always pronounced with an *l*)

Macloutsie: a military post in Bechuanaland

Mai Chaza: a woman who claimed to have risen from the dead to preach; founder of a religious sect known as 'Mayi Chaza'

Majaha: young men or young soldiers

Makalanga: a tribe which occupied most of Matebeleland before the arrival of the Matebele

Manicaland: the eastern area of Rhodesia; land of the Manyika people

Mashona, Mashonaland: term used to denote the Mazezuru, Makaranga, Manyika and Makorekore tribes and the area they occupied

Matebele, Matebeleland: the Europeanized form of the word 'Amandebele' from the Sesotho word 'litebele'—name given to Mzilikazi's people; Matebeleland is land occupied by Matebele

Matopo Hills: a group of hills not far from Bulawayo where Mlimu resided and where Mzilikazi and Rhodes are buried

Matshobana: Mzilikazi's father

Mondi: Maund

Mazezuru: a group of tribes in Central Mashonaland which forms one of the constituents of the Mashona people

Mbiko: commander of the Zwangendaba regiment which did not recognize Lobengula as king

Mfundisi: means teacher, synonymous with Reverend

Mlimu: God or Spirit worshipped by the Matebele

Mopane: type of tree

Nqwenya: clan surname of the people whose totem is the crocodile

Old Location: section of the African residential area of Bulawayo

Palapye: a village in Bechuanaland

Pathfinder: an organization identical with the Scout movement, so called in order to distinguish it from the Scout movement, membership of which was restricted to Europeans only

Selu: F. C. Selous, a famous hunter

Sindebele: language of the Amandebele people

Tati: an area on the border of Bechuanaland and Matebeleland

Tomusoni: Thompson, one of Rhodes' emissaries to Lobengula

Tshaka: king of the Zulu nation

Waddilove Mission: A Mission Station of the Methodist Missionary Society

Zansi: term used to distinguish those Matebele clans which came from Zululand—original home of the Matebele

Zoutpansberg: an area in the Northern Transvaal

Zwangendaba: a regiment led by Mbiko. Also name of a general of Tshaka who broke away from the Zulus and went north

Zwimba: one of the Mazezuru tribes living in the Lomagundi District of Sinoia whose ancestral area is called Chipata